Henry Peterson

Caesar

A Dramatic Study

Henry Peterson

Caesar
A Dramatic Study

ISBN/EAN: 9783337342975

Printed in Europe, USA, Canada, Australia, Japan

Cover: Foto ©Andreas Hilbeck / pixelio.de

More available books at **www.hansebooks.com**

CÆSAR;

A DRAMATIC STUDY.

By HENRY PETERSON,

Author of "The Modern Job," "Pemberton," &c.

PHILADELPHIA:

H. PETERSON & CO.,

1879.

CÆSAR;

A DRAMATIC STUDY.

IN FIVE ACTS.

BY

HENRY PETERSON,

Author of " The Modern Job," " Pemberton," &c.

———

———

PHILADELPHIA:

H. PETERSON & CO.

1879.

NOTICE.

"Any person publicly performing or representing any dramatic
composition for which a copyright has been obtained, without the
consent of the proprietor, or his heirs or assigns, shall be liable for
damages therefor; such damages in all cases to be assessed at such
sum, *not less* than one hundred dollars for the first, and fifty dollars
for every subsequent performance, as to the Court shall appear to be
just."—*Revised Statutes of the United States, Section* 4966.

PRICE, 50 CENTS.

PREFACE.

The popular idea of Julius Cæsar is derived from Shakspeare's admirable play. Shakspeare's conception of that great man's character was undoubtedly drawn from Plutarch. But recent historians have shown that there is another view to be taken of Cæsar. The freedom which Brutus and the other conspirators sought, was more probably the right of the aristocracy to rule as it pleased, than the establishment of those equal rights for all, which we term freedom in the present day.

I trust that I may not be deemed presumptuous in choosing the dramatic form in which to develope my conception of the character of Cæsar, and of the cruel and licentious times in which he lived. Of course only a certain amount of success can be my justification. And yet I cannot fairly be blamed for falling far behind the great master of dramatic literature. If his conception of Cæsar is essentially a mistaken one, owing to his want of adequate historical information, it does not seem to me overstepping the proper line of literary modesty, for modern authors to attempt a more correct personation, even if they should not possess a tithe of the genius of Shakspeare.

As to the question whether Brutus really was Cæsar's son, I may briefly say that it was a common belief at Rome; and I think the weight of the evidence is in favor of that belief. Of course it is sufficiently probable to allow of its reasonable use in a drama; which has the right to deal with history in a rather freer manner than the historian is compelled to observe.

I may add that the murder of Roscius and the divorce of Pompeia are in their essential facts historical.

THE AUTHOR.

CHARACTERS.

Caius Julius Cæsar.

Cornelius.................................A sage. Cæsar's friend.

Clodius.....................................A dissipated Roman noble.

Sextus......................................Friend and tool of Clodius.

Mark Antony.

Cicero.

Cassius ⎫
Brutus ⎪
Decimus ⎬ ....Conspirators.
Cimber ⎪
Casca ⎭

Roscius...A country gentleman.

Chrysogonus....................................Sylla's favorite freedman.

Sacula.......................................A leader of the mob.

Soothsayer.

Aurelia...Cæsar's mother.

Pompeia...Cæsar's wife.

Calpurnia......Cæsar's wife, after the divorce of Pompeia.

Abra ....Pompeia's maid.

Senators, Citizens, Soldiers, Vestal Virgins, &c.

CÆSAR;

A DRAMATIC STUDY.

ACT I.

PROSCRIBED BY SYLLA.

Scene I.—*A Street in Rome.*

Enter two Citizens.

First Cit. Yes, you say right, neighbor—these are terrible times! Half the people in rags; and thousands living in cellars.

Sec. Cit. And yet there's plenty of money; that is, for the nobles. They fling their silver about, as if it were copper or brass.

First Cit. It's just as bad in the country, too. No man can live any more by honest labor in Italy. He has to sell his little farm, and join the rest of us beggars in the towns.

Sec. Cit. Oh, that's because the great nobles with their gangs of slaves can undersell them. No free man will come down to a slave's long hours, and a slave's mean food, till he is absolutely forced to.

Enter Saculia.

Sacu. How now, masters, what are you conspiring about?

First Cit. (*Alarmed.*) Conspiring! We are not conspiring. We are honest citizens.

Sacu. You'd better be! There's a dozen more heads hanging in the Forum this morning. Old Mulberry must have had a bad dinner yesterday.

First Cit. Old Mulberry?

Sacu. Yes, old Sylla! His face looks more like a mulberry, sprinkled with white flour, than anything else. They say the reason his hair and his eyes are so red is, that he washes them in a bowl of fresh, warm blood every morning.

Second Cit. Aren't you afraid to talk thus? Remember that walls have ears.

5

Sacu. Oh, I know you. You belong to old Marius's party. You are friends of the people.

First Cit. We are honest, peaceable citizens, and do not meddle with political affairs.

Sec. Cit. Yes; they are above such as we are.

Sacu. (*Laughs.*) Oh, of course. But don't be afraid. Why you are not worth killing. Now if either of you had plenty of money—or a pretty house that some one wanted—or a pretty wife—why then I wouldn't give a drachma for his life from one day to another. But it is good to be poor sometimes. My head would have been off a month ago, only that my pockets are empty. (*Looks L.*) But who comes here? A countryman, I'll wager. Country people always walk like this—they are so used to stumbling over clods and stones. (*Mimics a countryman—lifting his feet very high*). Good morning, my worthy high-stepper—how's corn to-day?

Enter ROSCIUS, L.

Ros. Good friends. I am seeking the house of Tullius Magnus. Can you tell me the nearest way to reach it?

Sacu. What brings you to town? If I were outside a wolf's den, I would stay outside.

Ros. Magnus is my kinsman. Besides, he owes me some money, and wrote that if I would come to Rome, he should be greatly pleased to pay it.

(CITIZENS *smile.* SACULIA *bursts out laughing.*)

Sacu. Show him to me! Show me that man in Rome who wants to pay his debts! We will have him exhibited at the circus—and his statue erected in the Forum. Seriously, my good rural friend, more debts are being settled now with the point of the sword than in any other way. Are you rich?

Ros. Oh, no, not rich. But I have a very pretty little villa at Ameria. There is no harm in that, I hope?

Sacu. There is infinite harm in it. See here, my friend— what do you call yourself when at home?

Ros. My name is Sextus Roscius.

Sacu. Well, my good rural friend Roscius, take a fool's advice. Put a day's ride between you and these streets of Rome as soon as possible. I know your dear cousin Magnus—and that he is often seen in company with Chrysogonus, old Mulberry's favorite freedman. Take a friend's advice, my dear high-stepper, and say good-bye to Rome.

First Cit. Yes, 'tis wise counsel.

Sec. Cit. Numa couldn't have given better.

Ros. You frighten me. But my cousin expects me. Besides, I have never before been in Rome, and wanted to see something of the great city.

Sacu. If you had been here a few days since, you might have seen these streets of Rome spotted with bloody bodies. And now—if you stray as far as the Forum—you will see it strung around with human heads. It is a new style of ornament adopted in Rome of late. It's a head—if not a head and shoulders—above everything else.

Enter CHRYSOGONUS, *with Guards, R.*

Chry. Clear the way, you miscreants! What are you gathered here for? Planning new insurrections? Take care! or Sylla's sword, after the grain is reaped, may sweep down among the weeds.

Sacu. Weeds! well said, that! All Rome wears the blackest of weeds now.

Chry. Who are you that speak so boldly? Ah, Saculia, the leader of the mob! Well, you're a licensed jester. My master likes a joke; but still, take care!

Sacu. Yes, old Mulberry knows a good joke when he hears it. What did he say to you the other day in the Forum, when he heard me call him old Mulberry?

Chry. I asked him whether I should throw your head to the hogs.

Sacu. Very kind and neighborly that, to be sure! And what did Sylla answer?

Chry. That if we killed all the fools in Rome, there would be nobody left.

Sacu. That's true. Even you wouldn't be left then, good Chrysogonus. (*Citizens laugh.*)

Chry. (*To First Citizen, fiercely.*) And who are you, you grinning cur?

First Cit. I am only a poor shopkeeper.

Chry. A poor shopkeeper—a very poor one, I should think; who passes his time talking in the street, instead of attending to his business. And you complain of hard times too. (*To Second Citizen.*) And who are you?

Sec. Cit. I am an armorer—and an old soldier also.

Chry. Well, *you* have plenty of business.   Arms are always wanted.

Sec. Cit. Yes, my shop is swept clean at every fresh outbreak, whether of people or nobles.

Chry. That makes thy business lively.

Sacu. Yes, his arms and armor go off very lively; so lively that his customers generally forget to stop and pay for them.

Chry. (*To Roscius.*)   And who are you ?

Ros. I am a stranger in Rome.   My name is—

Sacu. (*Putting him aside.*)   He is an old friend of mine —from Capua.

Ros. (*In surprise.*)   No ; I am from Ameria.   And my name is Sextus Roscius.

Chry. (*Aside.*)   The very man !   (*To Roscius.*)   Well met, good Roscius.   I know thy kinsman Magnus.   He is to meet me this very hour in the Forum.

Ros. Indeed !   I was going to his house.

Chry. You had better come on to the Forum.   Shall I tell him you are coming?

Ros. Yes, if I can find some one to guide me.

Chry. (*To Saculia.*)   Buffoon, thou wilt guide him.   And play no tricks either on him, or me.   You will not fail me, good Roscius?

Ros. Oh no, I shall be there shortly.

Chry. (*To Citizens.*)   As for you, fellows—you come too. That you may see who's master now in Rome.

(*Exeunt* CHRYSOGONUS *and Guards, L.*)

Ros. What great Senator is that?   My cousin seems to fly high in Rome.

Sacu. Great Senator!   (*Laughs.*)   Oh thou quintessence of rural innocence !   That is Chrysogonus, old Sylla's favorite freedman.

Ros. A freedman !

Sacu. Oh, all kinds of fowls wear eagle's feathers nowadays.   Better have the ill-will of half the senators of Rome, than of old Mulberry's freed slave.   And now, get thee home to Ameria as fast as thy old horse can foot it.

Ros. Why I have just promised, as you heard, to meet my kinsman in the Forum.

Sacu. Promised!   Wouldst thou keep a promise to meet a hungry tiger in his jungle ?

Ros. Yes, if I had made it.   Whatever may be the new

fashion in Rome, he has the word of an Italian gentleman.

Sacu. He means thee no good. I could see that in his false eyes, hear it in his false voice.

Ros. Why, what harm can he mean me? I have lived quietly on my farm—have had nothing to do with politics—have taken no side, either with Marius or Sylla.

Sacu. So said the innocent sheep to the wolf. "I have never harmed thee," said the sheep. "I do not mean to eat thee because thou hast harmed me; but because thou art fat," said the wolf. Go home, Roscius—secrete thyself for a while—and die in thy bed.

Ros. I have given him my word—and I have harmed no one. Secure in my innocence, I fear no wolf in Rome.

First Cit. Oh that old Marius were alive again!

Sec. Cit. All the old leaders of the people are dead; and none are left to fill their places.

Sacu. Wait a while, and the young sprouts will grow. There is Marius's nephew, young Julius Cæsar. He's got the right stuff in him, or I'm no judge of sword-fish.

First Cit. What!—that idle, dissolute young Cæsar?

Sacu. Wait a while. The fire is crackling and wavering yet; but watch and see if before long, it does not begin to burn with a bright and steady flame.

Sec. Cit. Ah, would we had a young man now like Tiberius or Caius Gracehus.

Sacu. What, to be killed off in a few years as they were? We need something of wilier, sterner make to suit these times. But come, friend Roscius—if you really intend to keep your foolish promise. You'll see a sight in the Forum that will show you how the avenging Furies are raging now in Rome. Come—this way! Hold, one caution! When you get to the Forum, don't you either laugh or cry at what you see there. They killed one man for crying the other day; and then, when another man laughed, they killed him for laughing. Come!

(*Exeunt* SACULIA *and* ROSCIUS, *L.*)

First Cit. Let us go too. It is about the hour the new lists of proscription are posted. Whose turn comes next I wonder. (*Exeunt* CITIZENS, *L.*)

1*

SCENE II.—*The Forum.   The Rostrum with a number of
human heads strung around it.*

Enter CICERO *and* CÆSAR.

Cic. Oh, horrible sight!   The noblest heads in Rome
Brought here to be the sport and ridicule
Of a vile mob of freedmen and of slaves! .
Cæs. Who can say now it is the mob are cruel?
My uncle Marius I own, my friend,
Was not renowned for mercy ; and his sword
Stopped not its slaughter when the battle ceased,
As swords of brave men should ; but he was mild
As a young lamb, compared to this red wolf
Who rages now in Rome.   Sylla, the pet
And leader of the nobles!   Sylla, chief
Of those who proudly call themselves "the best!"
Sylla, the beast, the wolf, the murderer!
Cic. Speak lower, Cæsar.   Know you not these stones
Have ears?   For less—far less—than those few words
Poor Lucius was condemned.
Cæs.   Curses upon
His red-eyed slayer!   If the assassin's blade
Were ever rightful—
Cic.   Hush! be careful, Cæsar!
You know he loves you not too well already.
Cæs. I ought to know.   He took my priesthood too,
Yesterday morn.
Cic.   That was because you failed
To obey his will, and marry as he bade.
Cæs. Yes, we must marry now, as well as die,
To suit the tyrant's pleasure.   Did you hear
The dowry of my wife was taken too?
Cic. Take care then, Cæsar ; you'll have nothing left
For him to take soon but your precious life.
Cæs. Four thousand men—the noblest souls in Rome—
Men of the gentlest breeding ; scholars, statesmen—
Five hundred Senators, the choicest spirits
Of this our wretched time, all now lie low
Beneath this butcher's sword.   What was their crime?
Because they loved the people—saw them ground
Into the mire, beneath the cruel wheels
Of the rapacious nobles—saw their farms
Torn from their hands by either force or fraud—

Saw the stout soldiers who had fought for Rome
In scores of battles, turned in their old age
Out in the streets to die, as you would turn
An old horse on the common—and, seeing this,
Vowed they would make things better, and bring back
The good Rome of our fathers, where no man,
Honest and brave, could ever fail of bread.

Cic. Beware, my friend, the Gracchi reasoned thus—
And perished!

Cœs. Yes, and from their sacred dust,
Scattered in scorn upon this Roman air,
A Marius sprang*—who did not bow his head
So meekly to the butchers, but struck back
With blows that make bad men remember yet.

Cic. But now the luck is changed. Who are these coming?

Cœs. Why it is Clodius. You don't like the man?

Cic. Like him! gay, reckless, idle, dissolute,—
I wonder much that you can call him friend.

Cœs. Oh, I am not myself a paragon.
My blood still runs too hotly in my veins.
And yet I do not pride myself upon
My want of strength, as our young nobles do.
But Clodius, whate'er faults he may have,
Has this one virtue, that he loves the people.
For me I love all men who are my friends,
And serve the people's cause.

Enter CLODIUS *and* SEXTUS.

Clo. Is that you, Cæsar?
By all the gods who love a merry life,
Why have you kept yourself so close of late?

Cœs. Are these safe times to go much out of doors?

Clo. Oh, if you once begin to think such thoughts,
No pleasure's left in life. Life's dull enough
Without our making it more dull by moping.
You should have been with us last night. Oh, Phœbus,
What sport we had!—had we not, Sextus mine?

Sex. In faith you may say that. For first we danced
Until our legs gave out—and then we drank
Until our throats gave out—and then we reeled
Into the streets, and (*sinks voice*) broke from off their bodies
Some of the prettiest marble heads in Rome.

---

*"The mother of the Gracchi cast the dust of her murdered sons into the⸺
air, and out of it sprung Caius Marius." *Mirabeau.*

Clo. The statues, you know. It is the fashion now
To take off heads in Rome ; and so we followed
The fashion, Cæsar. Was it not well thought?
    Cœs. Whose statues were they?
    Clo.   Some of fat old Sylla,
And some of Scipio, and other ancients.
All were, however, of the other side ;
For though it's no harm to be drunk, a man
Should never be so drunk as not to know
Who are his friends. But where were you last night,
My worthy Cæsar?
    Cœs.   With my mother, Clodius.
    Clo. Oh no, my Cæsar—that's too good a boy.
If you had said, somebody else's mother,
I might have thought it true. The fair Servilia—
    Cœs. Pardon me, Clodius! Think you are my friend.
Servilia is old Brutus' honored wife.
And we were boy and girl together when
She married him, as ladies do in Rome,
Because her father willed it. Not a breath
Must touch her fame, spoken by friend of mine.
    Clo. Let it pass, Cæsar. All my faith was lost
In women years ago. And still I held
There are a few Lucretias left in Rome.
    Sex. (*Laughs.*) Yes, that is true. There are four of us
      here ;—
There are four virtuous women left in Rome,
And each of us has one. As for the rest!

                          (*He flings up his hands.*)

    Cic. There was a time when, for three hundred years,
In Rome's first days, no woman false was found,
And no man false to woman !
    Clo.   Oh, great Bacchus!
Life must have been intolerably dull.
    Sex. No stabbings—no divorce—no jumpings o'er
The garden walls! I'm glad I was not born
When women were so good.
    Cœs.   So am not I !
Oh, Cicero, had I breathed purer air,
What might I not have been? The fruit must grow
Bitter or sweet, as is the parent bough.
'Tis in me to be noble. But, alas !

My friends must take young Cæsar as the world
Has fashioned him, nor blame too much his faults.

Cic. Here comes Chrysogonus, with the red list
Of the proscribed. Were it not safer, friends,
To leave at once? For no man here can tell
Whether or not his fated name is down
Upon the tyrant's blood-roll.

Clo.   I'll not run,
Like a scared rat. Ev'n Sylla will think twice
Before he lays his hand upon a Claudius.

Cæs. Nor I. Sylla can do no more than Fate
Allows him. Cæsar was not born to die,
Before his time, like some poor village boy.
Fear not, my friends, for Destiny has arms
Stronger than Sylla's.

Enter, R, CHRYSOGONUS with Guards—and goes to the Rostrum. Guards range themselves. Enter also, L, SACULIA, ROSCIUS and CITIZENS.

Chry. (Ascends Rostrum.) The list of the proscribed is
    short to-day.
Great Sylla's heart is growing merciful.

Sacu. (Aside.) Just as a man grows tired of eating, when
He's had a pig or two. (*To Chry.*) Bless his kind soul!

CHRYSOGONUS *produces a scroll, and begins to read.*

Chry. (Reads.) "The following citizens are doomed to
    death.
All persons are forbid to harbour them,
Or give them food or shelter, under pain
Also of death. Whoever brings the head
Of either of them to the Capitol,
Shall have for his reward ten thousand drachmas.
Witness my seal.

                              Sylla the Fortunate,
                              Dictator of the World."

Clo. (Aside.) There's modesty! Now let us hear the
    names.

Chry. (Reads.) "This is the list of the proscribed:—
Quintillus Publicola, Lucius Aurelius,
And Sextus Roscius of Ameria."

Ros. (Horror-struck.) Not I! not I! I have no enemies.
I take no part in politics. Good friends,
'Tis a mistake! Some other man is meant.

CHRYSOGONUS *descends from Rostrum, and draws his sword.*
Guards inclose ROSCIUS.

Chry. Thou liest, knave! Thou art a secret plotter
With all the vilest elements of Rome.
What dost thou here in company with curs
Like this Saculia—this leader vile ,
Of the vile mob—whom we let live awhile
Only because his life's not worth the taking?
Wretch! Thou shalt die at once. Don't be a child!
Die at least like a Roman.
　　Ros.　　　　　　　Save me, friends!

(*Breaks through Guards, and flings himself before Cæsar*
and his friends.)

Save me, great Senators! There's some mistake.
I know there is. I take no part in plots.
I am a simple farmer of Ameria,
Come here to see the city, and collect
A debt that's due me. Save me, Senators!
　　Cæs. There must be some mistake, Chrysogonus.
This man is not a plotter. Hold thy hand,
Till Sylla's will is known; and hold him too,
That he may not escape. Have pity, man!
　　Chry. And dare you, Cæsar, interfere between
Great Sylla and his victims! Know you not
The fearful penalty for shielding those
Who are proscribed? This man's an arrant knave.
I know him to be guilty.
　　Sacu. (*Aside.*)　　　Not a doubt
He's guilty of possessing something nice
That this Chrysogonus wants—the cruel wretch!
　　Chry. Back, plotter! Lies can now no longer save thee!

(*He seizes* ROSCIUS, *and drags him back among the Guards.*)

　　Cæs. (*Starts forward.*) Now, by the eternal Gods!
　　Cic.　　　　　　　　Be calm, my friend,
Put not yourself in peril. See you not,
You can do nothing now? If wrong is done,
The laws of Rome will some day right the man.
　　Cæs. The law can never bring the dead to life—
Once life is gone, then comes eternal night.
I cannot stand and see the innocent
Thus slaughtered 'fore my eyes.

Clo. Patience, my friend.
We can do nothing now. When our turn comes,
We then can take due vengeance for this wrong.
   Ros. No one will help me? Oh, my wife, my child!
Why did I enter this accursed Rome?
   Chry. What, and you dare blaspheme! Take this! and
      this! (*Stabs* ROSCIUS.)
   Ros. (*Falls.*) My wife! my child! (*Dies.*)
   Chry. (*To Guards.*) Ten thousand drachmas more, my
      boys! These times
Will make us all as rich as Midas was.
For all that we touch, too, with the sharp points
Of our good swords, turns straightway into gold.
   Clo. Well, are the day's diversions over now,
My good Chrysogonus? If so, we'll go.
   Chry. By no means. The best part is yet to come.
There was one name that I forgot to read.

Goes on Rostrum, and takes up list.

That name—it is the last and yet the greatest—
Is Caius Julius Cæsar! What think you—
Does not the play grow prettier towards the close?
               (*Chry. and Guards laugh.*)
   Cæs. (*Starts.*) Ha!
   Clo. (*To Cæs.*) Rush for your life! Sextus and I will
      block
The soldiers' way. Fear not for us, but go!
        (*Cicero falls away a little from Cæsar.*)
   Cic. Do not resist the law, my friend. Be sure
That soon or late the law will do you justice!
I'll give my life to that!
   Cæs. (*Smiles grimly.*) Thanks, Cicero!
But where shall I be then? I was not born
To die by a slave's sword.
       CHRYSOG. *and Guards approach with drawn swords.*
   Chry. (*Holds out point of sword to Cæs.*) Here is my
      sword,
Most noble Cæsar. Will you run upon it?
You hear the doom of Sylla. Being a Roman,
You do not fear to die.
   Cæs. When Marius
Was fleeing from his foes in Africa,
A slave like thee, Chrysogonus, one day

Menaced his breast with his uplifted steel.
"Who art thou," cried the hero, "that dost dare
To raise his hand 'gainst Caius Marius!"
.And now I ask, How dar'st thou, graceless wretch,
To menace me, great Marius's nephew?
    Chry. I know that I am nothing of myself.
But I am everything as Sylla's arm—
Sylla, to whom great Marius was a child.
Prepare to die, then, Cæsar, 't is thy fate.
    Cæs. (*Calmly*) I have no thought of dying in this hour,
My part Chrysogonus. The Augurs said,
When I was priest of Jupiter, that death
Should never touch this frame, till I was sworn
First Consul. More, they said the man that slew me
Should not survive my death over three days.
    Clo. I'll take my oath on that!
    Sacu.   And so will I!
    Cæs. I judge the Augurs knew that I had friends
Who would not suffer such a wretch to live
More than three days. What good is money then,
When thou canst not enjoy it?
    Chry.   But my duty
As Sylla's officer. That must be done.
    Cæs. Can Sylla's warrant pluck thee from the tomb?
Thou seest now, it is not quite so small
And light a thing to hunt and kill a Cæsar.
—What are you wolves to get for killing me?
    Chry. Ten thousand drachmas!
    Cæs.   What! no more than that!
No more than for a common, worthless knave!
Ten thousand drachmas only for a Cæsar!
Sylla is growing mean! Why I will give
Five times ten thousand drachmas as a gift
To you and these brave soldiers, who no doubt
Have flown our eagles on a hundred fields
From Parthia to Spain.
        (CHRYSOGONUS *looks at Guards, who nod assent.*)
    Chry.   Give me the money!
And for to-day, count thyself safe from us.
To-morrow, we will hunt thee, yea or nay.
        (CÆSAR *takes out tablets and writes on one.*)
    Cæs. Take this to-morrow to my mother's house,
And she will pay you.

Chry.   What security
Have you to give we shall not be betrayed?
Clo. I will secure it you.
Cæs.   No, thank you, Clodius.
The word of Cæsar is enough in Rome,
And they shall have no other. What, thou slave,
Dost thou pretend to talk to Caius Cæsar
About security—as if he were
Some vile usurer? Know that Cæsar's word
Once broke, Cæsar is dead—more truly dead
Than if his heart were cloven with your swords!
Take this, and hand it to my mother—she
Will pay you every drachma of my bond.

                           (*Chry. takes it.*)

     Chry. (*To Guards.*) A good day's work, my noble veterans.
Mark—fifty thousand drachmas—sixty in all!
Cæsar, to-morrow, we will hunt and kill thee,
And earn ten thousand more—if Pluto wills.

     Cæs. Fair warning is it, good Chrysogonus!
I give thee warning too. The time will come
When I shall stand in this red Sylla's place.
Then thou shalt plead for mercy. Mark me now!
I will not spare thee, though thy wife and mother
Beseech me on their knees. Thou and thy scum
Of slaves and freedmen all shall surely die!
For while you live you outrage Gods and men.
Come on, my friends. My time is precious now.

                           (*Exeunt.*)

END OF ACT I.

ACT II.

THE DIVORCE OF POMPEIA.

SCENE I.—*A Street in Rome.*

Enter SACULIA.

Sacu. (*Looks around.*) Well, things look natural enough again in Rome. One might think the whole city would go to the dogs, just because he had left for awhile. It's curious how the world always manages to get along so well without us.

Enter First CITIZEN.

Hallo, neighbor!—glad to see you're still kicking this dirty old earth with your stampers.

First Cit. Why, Saculia, where have you been? I've not seen you for many a day.

Sacu. No, I suppose not. In fact I thought after that affair in the Forum, I had better retire to one of my country houses for awhile, as the other big bugs do. I thought the weather was getting rather too warm in Rome.

First Cit. Ah, that was a very sad affair—that murder of poor Roscius. But there's one good thing—his son has got the property back again.

Sacu. Yes, I heard that Cicero had prosecuted Chrysogonus, and got the property back. There's some good left in the lawyers yet—if you'll only pay them big enough fees, and elect them to all the fat offices.

First Cit. I suppose when old Sylla died, you thought you might come back again.

Sacu. Oh, I was in no hurry. I rather liked the country. That old wretch Sylla—did you ever hear how he died?

First Cit. I suppose in the usual way—shortness of breath, or something of that sort.

Sacu. Yes, that's true. But one of his slaves told me all about it. What with his feasting and drinking, and his loose women, he grew rottener and rottener every day. Until at last he was fairly eaten up by worms. They washed him three times a day, but 'twas no use—they couldn't keep him clean of the lice and worms. Fit end, wasn't it, for such a bloody old tyrant? I tell you, my friend, the philosophers may say what they choose, but the Furies, with their whips of Scorpious, aren't all dead yet.

. *First Cit.* No, indeed, neighbor—we couldn't get along well without them. A man may be too rich and strong for the laws in this world, but at the end of life, he will have to meet the Furies.

Sacu. And Cæsar is back too, I hear ;—Prætor and Pontifex Maximus, and carrying all before him. Hurra for Cæsar, the friend of the people! But good day, neighbor ; I have a host of old friends to see. Ah, are you going my way ?   (*Exeunt, L.*)

Enter CLODIUS *and* SEXTUS, *R.*

Clo. Oh, the beautiful Pompeia! What else did Abra say ?

Sex. She said that Pompeia would give you an interview this evening—if you had the nerve and daring to attempt it.

Clo. Nerve! daring! Thou told'st her I'd stop at nothing, short of meeting her in Cæsar's presence? That I own is more than I'd like to do. There is something in Cæsar's eyes when he is roused, that even I, Sextus, do not always care to meet.

Sex. And yet a little spice of danger makes an adventure all the pleasanter.

Clo. Of course—of course! I really believe it is because Pompeia is so jealously guarded—as if she were the golden fruit within the gardens of the Hesperides—that I so long to kiss her sweet lips. But how shall we manage to evade that terrible mother-in-law? Dear Sextus, tell me how.

Sex. To-night you know is the great festival of Bona Dea —that mysterious goddess brought from the East, which it is the ruling fashion now for all our great ladies to worship.

Clo. Oh yes, but they will not allow a single male—married or unmarried—to remain in the house where their mysterious rites are carried on.

Sex. Would you not like to witness those rites which are .....
kept so secret ?

Clo. Indeed I should. The whole thing is outrageous. It is an insult to every man in Rome. Of course we men

do not care that our wives should have their little mysteries;—it is the keeping them from their husbands that is
so unwifely and abominable. But how, Sextus? Some of
these ladies, it is said, carry poniards on such occasions—
and would not hesitate to use them too. And it is bad
enough to be killed, without being laughed at afterwards as
the man that was poniarded by a pack of crazy women.
They'd soon have it in the Forum that I had been pricked
to death by the women's knitting needles.

Sex. Abra has planned all that. You must go disguised
as a woman. Not every man could do that, Clodius,—but
you could.

Clo. I think I could. I tricked some ladies famously a
year or so ago, dressed in my sister's garments.

Sex. You must not speak though. Your voice would at
once betray you. Remember that!

Clo. Oh, mum's the word. But how shall I see Pompeia?

Sex. You enter boldly. Abra will be near the door.
She will lead you as soon as she can get an opportunity to
Pompeia's own sitting room; where, as soon as possible, the
fair dame will join you. By Venus, I wish it was myself,
and not you, my Clodius.

Clo. It is well planned. I'll try to find out too, what
those secret rites are that the ladies of Rome are so fond of.
I hope that I shall not meet Cæsar, though; his keen eyes
would see through my disguise at a glance.

Sex. He would be angry enough to kill you.

Clo. Not at all. You do not know Cæsar. His marriage
with Pompeia was merely a matter of policy. Besides, I
am too necessary to him; for any moment he may break
with Pompey. He has great plans to rejuvenate old Rome,
and will allow no private griefs to come between him and
his purpose.

Sex. Well, it is worth some risk to meet so fine a woman!
Do you go this morning to the Forum?

Clo. No, I must go and make ready my attire. My sister
will think it the best of sport to help me, and trig me out
as a grand Roman dame. Good day.

Sex. Good day—and Venus give you luck!

                                   (*Exeunt R. and L.*)

Scene II.—*Hall in Cæsar's house (the palace of the Pontifex Maximus.)*

Enter Aurelia.

Aure. We mothers of Rome scarce dwell a day in peace
What man in Rome, worthy the name of man,
But bears his life in daily, hourly hazard?
Rome slaughters always those who love her best,
And strive to make her prosperous and great.
Thus fell Tiberius and Caius Gracchus,
Cornelia's brilliant jewels. What their crime?
Only they loved the people—pitied the poor—
And sought to curb the selfish greed of gain
Of Rome's proud nobles, so the poor might live.
And now my Caius steps the self-same path,
I trust with firmer tread. He is a noble;
But, as the nobles say, false to his order.
Yes, false to them, but true to heaven and Rome!
But it is time he came. Ah, that is he.

Enter Cæsar.

Cæs. My noble mother! (*Kisses her.*)
Aure. My Caius! Thou art late.
Cæs. Yes, state affairs pressed more than usual. Ah,
Sometimes I wish I were a villager,
And had no thought save of my pigs and cows.
It is no pleasure, mother, to rule men.
They are more obstinate than pigs or cows,
And far more apt to turn and gore their ruler.
Aure. Men were not born for pleasure; but to work
The will of the great gods. Each in his place,
Where they have put him, finds his destined task.
He cannot shun that task and be a man
Worthy the name of man, much less of Cæsar.
Cæs. 'Tis true, my mother. I have not forgot
Thy noble teachings. But the task sometimes
Seems doubly hard. No matter. This is folly.
Where is Pompeia?
Aure. She seems vexed to-day.
Why didst thou give that costly pearl of thine,
That pearl unmatched in Rome or in the world,
To Brutus' wife, Servilia? Was't well done,
My Caius? All the drawing rooms of Rome
Are babbling over it.

Cæs.   Let the fools babble!

Aure. I ask again, Was it well done, my Caius?

Cæs. If any other tongue in Rome had put
That question to me, I would turn and say
It *was* well done—and bid them hold their peace.
Thou art my mother; and I bow my head,
As when I was a boy, here at thy knee,
And say: 'Twas *not* well done—nor fitting Cæsar.
                    (*Sits down at his mother's feet.*)

Aure. I pain thee, Caius. But, my noble son,
I wound as surgeons do, only to heal.
That pearl of thine Servilia 'll wash with dew,
And lay it in the sun, to make it glow
With added lustre. Thou my pearl art, Caius!
I have no jewel but thee. And I would wash
Thee with my tears, and hang thee in the sun
Of heaven's great eye, if so thou might'st become
Purer and nobler ev'n than thou art now.

Cæs. Bear with me, mother. Gems sometimes have flaws
That go down to their hearts. You can outroot
The fatal flaw only by shattering
The gem to pieces.

Aure.   Is it so bad as that?

Cæs. We marry now in Rome, not whom we love,
But whom we must. That is the great lords do,
Who seek for power to spoil or save the state.
Pompeia is Pompey's cousin as you know.
Servilia married by her father's order,
Old Marcus Brutus. Thus we give our hands,
Both men and women, as ambition wills.
But hearts are different things, and will not be
Thus coldly given to order. And I love
Only one woman in Rome.

Aure.   And her name is?

Cæs. Servilia.

Aure.   Still it was not wise, my son,
To set all Rome thus talking.

Cæs.   'Twas unwise.
Yet they had talked, and talked, till they were hoarse,
Of that affair already. Besides, where all
Are guilty, who can have the face to peep
Into his neighbour's windows, and make mouths,
Without himself accusing? All are the same.

Ev'n Cato, who aspires to lead the van,
Aud be a moral pattern to all Rome,
Has given, you know, his wife unto his friend,
Though she has borne him children. And, mark this—
If ever his friend should die, and leave her rich,
Your virtuous Cato 'll take her back again!
Ah, times have changed, my mother, since the day
When Manlius was banished from the Senate,
For kissing his wife before his daughter's eyes.
The bow thus drawn too tight, has since then broken.
But where's Pompeia? I wish much to see her.
   Aure. Well, here she comes.

(*Enter* POMPEIA *slowly. She takes no notice of* CÆSAR, *but goes to one side.*)

   Cæs.   Pompeia, I've a word
To say to you.
     Pom.   Say on! About pearls perhaps?
     Cæs. (*Frowns.*) No, of your maiden, Abra.
     Pom.   What of her?
Does she not please my lord? I'll try to find
A fairer maiden for him.
     Cæs.   Cease this jesting!
Abra was seen last night iu company
With Sextus Claudius. It is not fitting.
     Pom. Why, is he not a friend of Clodius?
And is not Clodius a close friend of yours?
     Cæs.   He is a tool of Clodius—and therefore
If Abra meet him, it but gives the vile
A chance to slander you.
     Pom.   To slander me?
How can that be? Could Cæsar's wife meet harm
From Cæsar's friend? Cæsar must have poor friends,
To harm his wife. Were it not well, my lord,
You chose such friends, women as well as men,
As slander on such poor and paltry grounds
Could not assail and cling to?
     Cæs.   We demand,
And rightly, purer lives from women than men.
Men bear the brunt of war, the toils of life;
A thousand ills assail them daily, which
You ladies of high rank are shielded from.
Your part in life is simply to direct

Your households, live in peace in pleasant homes,
And make yourselves as happy as you can.
One thing, in due return, is all we ask:
That we may warm no serpents at our hearths.

Pom. I'll give you, Cæsar, a sure recipe,
By which you may insure a virtuous wife
To every man in Rome.

Cæs.   And what is that?

Pom. Let every man be virtuous !

Cæs.   True, Pompeia !
And virtuous wives will bring that time about.
It is the woman's task to set a mark,
Which she first reaching, shall hold out her hand
To aid the man to strive for and attain.

Aure. Pompeia, having heard your wish, will see
To Abra's doings, Cæsar.

Pom. (*Aside.*) You old dragon !
I'll do as I please—as I have always done—
And as the other Roman ladies do.
If he divorces me—why, all the better !
I'd like another husband.   Tullia
Is not as old as I, and she has had
Three husbands now already.

Aure. Have you remembered, Cæsar, that to-night
Is the grand festival of Bona Dea ?
Not a male soul, be he or young or old,
Must stay within this house.   The vestal virgins,
And all the noblest ladies of our Rome
Will take part in the holy mysteries
With which we worship the Good Mother of all
This fruitful earth—from whose abounding womb
Spring fruits and flowers and all the precious grains,
And women and men—perhaps ev'n the great Gods !

Cæs. I've given strict orders.   No one shall profane
Your sacred mysteries.   I will myself
Be near at hand, in case some scoffing cur
Of these irreverent times, should dare disturb
Your pious rites with his blasphemous tongue

Aure. Thank thee, my son.   And now I judge, Pom
     peia,
Our evening meal is ready.   Shall we go ?

Cæs. I am quite ready, too.   I'll lead thee, mother.
Pompeia will excuse me?

Pom.   With pleasure, Cæsar.
(*Aside.*) There go the male and female dragon! Bah!

(*Exeunt* CÆSAR *leading his mother by the hand.* POMPEIA
following.)

SCENE III.—*Passage in* CLODIUS'S *house.*

Enter CLODIUS, ABRA *and* SEXTUS. CLODIUS *in female
attire.*

Clo. (*To Abra.*) The beautiful Pompeia then still wishes
me to come in spite of Cæsar's suspicions?

Abra. Oh yes; she thinks it only adds to the sport.

Sex. If he finds it out, he will divorce her.

Abra. She doesn't care. She says there's as good fish in
the sea as Cæsar.

Clo. Thou'rt a pretty minx. (*Kisses her.*)

Abra. You'd better keep your kisses for my mistress.
She's not had many of late. Cæsar's as cold as an icicle.

Clo. The wretch! But I've got plenty for you both.
For since I got these feminine garments on, I feel just the
same passion for kissing that all women do. I don't think
I can keep from kissing all the women there—even to the
vestal virgins.

Sex. Pray, my Clodius, do not touch the vestals. That's
a burning matter, you know. Shame on such old superstitions!

Clo. Oh, I'll let the sacred vestals alone. Half of them
are as sacred as parchment cheeks and a bad breath can
make them. But how do I look, Abra? Will I pass
muster?

ABRA *turns him around—and inspects him critically.*

Abra. Keep down your head and your eyes. Your dress
is all right. Stay—I'll fix this.

Clo. Oh, hold on!—you're hurting me!

Abra. That's of no consequence—so you look right. No
woman cares how much she hurts herself, when looks are
in question. Now let me see you walk.

CLODIUS *walks—taking long strides.*

Abra. Not such big steps. Go mincing along, so.
                     (*Shows him.* CLODIUS *imitates her.*)

Clo. How will that do? If I had only thought of tying

2

my legs together with a strap, it would have kept me in mind.

Abra. Oh, you'll do pretty well. Now, can you keep your mouth shut?

Clo. I don't know. Since I've been made a woman, I feel prodigiously like talking all the time—whether I have anything to say or not.

Abra. Bah! Women can be quiet enough when they wish to. Not a man in Rome knows what goes on at the women's worship of Bona Dea.

Sex. That's true, Abra. It's wonderful—very wonderful —but it's true! Even I don't know.

Clo. I'll tell you to-morrow, Sextus.

Sex. Half the men in Rome are dying to know. And so, if you are found out, they will all be disposed to shelter you from punishment, as an unlucky soldier in a good cause.

Abra. Well, I must go. I'll be on the watch for you.

(*Exit* ABRA, *L.*)

Sex. If Cæsar should divorce Pompeia, why then you can marry her.

Clo. Hem! not exactly! In truth, while I like spices as a condiment, I should not like to make my whole dinner of spices. Besides, Sextus, while I am not exactly a pattern of propriety myself, I think I should rather like my wife to be a pattern.

Sex. Oh, of course, that's human nature.

Clo. Yes, it's natural. Come this way, Sextus. This is the kind of woman I mean to marry.

(*Exit, R., primly—followed by* SEXTUS—*both laughing.*)

SCENE IV.—*Hall in* CÆSAR'S *Palace as before—but lighted and decorated for celebration.*

Enter AURELIA *and* POMPEIA.

Aure. Are all the inner chambers ready?

Pom.　　　　　　　　　　　　　　　　　Yes,
They all are decorated for the rites.
And the white doves are panting for the knife.
Where's Abra! Have you seen her?

Aure.　　　　　　　　　　　　　She came in
Just now in haste. She gads too much, Pompeia.
Speak to her sharply.

Pom.　　　　　　　That I will, good mother.

(*Calls.*) Abra!

Enter ABRA.

What mean you, Abra, by this gadding?
(*Takes her one side.*)
Will he be here?
  Abra.   By Venus, you may think so!
He is as mad with love as a spring sparrow.
He's in over his head. A pretty dame
He's made himself—ev'u handsomer than his sister.
  Pom. I'll eat him, pretty boy! Bring him at once
Into my parlour. You will find me there.
I've locked it, to keep curious meddlers out.
(*To Aurelia.*)   I go to see that all is right within.
(*Exit* POMPEIA.)
  Aure. Ah, here they come.

Enter Procession of VESTAL VIRGINS *in white, with tapers
in their hands, headed and attended by* PRIESTESSES *in
black; and followed by Roman ladies. Procession marches
around the hall singing.*

Song.

Bona Dea! gracious mother!
  Low we worship at thy shrine.
Hear our prayers, oh Bona Dea,
  Goddess holy and divine!
While we heap upon thy altar,
  Bread and fruit, and flesh and wine.
Hear us, goddess, lest we die!
Hear us, goddess, lest we die!

Bona Dea! grant us women
  All our hearts are keen to know.
Gracious mother! men are cruel,
  We lie trampled, crushed and low!
Bona Dea, be thou near us,
  In our hours of bitter woe!
Hear us, goddess, lest we die!
Hear us, goddess, lest we die!

Exit Procession, singing, into inner chambers of Palace.

  Aure. Follow the ladies, Abra. They may need thee.
I will stay here, and welcome those that come.

Abra. My mistress bade me not to leave this place;
And left a message with me.
Aure.   And I bid
That thou shouldst go within!
Abra. (*Aside.*)   I must at once
Go to Pompeia, and despatch her here,
Or there'll be trouble.   (*Exit* ABRA.)

Enter CLODIUS *in dress of Roman lady.* AURELIA *looks
at him sharply, and approaches him, but he evades her.*

Aure. That looks like Claudia—Clodius's sister;—
And yet a trifle tall, and somewhat older.
No, it's not she!
Clo. (*Aside.*) By Mercury, and all unlucky gods!
There's the she-wolf that guards the sacred fruit;
But where is Abra? Has she played me false?

Enter POMPEIA. *She glances at* CLODIUS, *and then goes to*
AURELIA.

Pom. Dear mother, I will now relieve thy charge.
Our friends will miss thee at the sacred rites.
Aure. In a few moments I will join them there.
                    (*She still observes* CLODIUS.)

                    (*Pompeia goes to Clodius.*)

Pom. Ah, Claudia, is it thou? I will conduct
Thee to the inner rooms. (*Aside.*) Take shorter steps!

Enter two PRIESTESSES *from within.*

First Priestess. Aurelia, we await thy coming. All
Is now prepared to make the sacrifice.
                    (*Aurelia steps before Clodius.*)
Aure. Why, Claudia, is it thou? How strange thou
            look'st.
What is the matter?
Pom. Claudia has taken a vow she will not speak
Till these great rites are over. Come, my dear.

*They take a few steps—*CLODIUS *forgetting himself, and taking long strides.*

Aure. That is not Claudia. Claudia walks not thus.
Ah, now I know her. That is Clodius.
Clodius! Pompeia! Shame upon you both!

First Priestess. A man! a man! Treason! oh sacred
goddess!

Sec. Priestess. A man! a wolf! (*To Pompeia.*) Oh, shameless woman thou!

False to thy husband—falsest to thy sex!

Enter ABRA. *Also* VESTAL VIRGINS, *with ladies, in alarm
and indignation.*

Aurelia. (*To Abra.*) Go tell thy master that I wish his
presence.   (*Exit* ABRA, *reluctantly.*)

Sec. Priestess. Behold the traitor and her paramour!
Who dare profane the rites of Bona Dea!
(*To Clodius.*) Blasphemer, death by fire were far too good
For thy deserts!

First Priestess. Make an example of him!
Let's sacrifice the wretch upon the altar
Of mighty Bona Dea! Let him feel
That Roman matrons can avenge their wrongs,
Without the aid of men! Come, sisters, on him!

The PRIESTESSES *pull out daggers. All gather around* CLO-
DIUS, *and pull his false hair off, and tear his garments.*

Clo. Bless me, fair ladies, but your claws are sharp.
Be off, you cats! Come now, have mercy! What!
You'll spit me with your daggers? No, by Pluto!
That goes too far. Aurelia, will you see
Me murdered 'fore your eyes by these she-tigers?

Aure. I have sent word to Cæsar. When he comes
He doubtless will protect you. Could he tell
That you were Clodius till your borrowed plumes
Were stripped from off your bold, audacious front?

Clo. Oh I'm not anxious that your son should know
To whom he is indebted for this rumpus.
It's not Pompeia's fault, but mine. She thought
I was my sister Claudia.

First Priestess.   Oh, of course!
                    (*All the ladies laugh.*)

Pom. Laugh on, you hussies, so it pleases you.
Clodius is wrong. I knew him from the first.
But, in my woman's heart, I could not think
To bring dishonor on my husband's friend,
Ev'n though his impious prying into rites
With which he'd naught to do, deserved all blame.

I meant to lead him off—tell him I saw
Through his disguise—and send him home in peace.
You, mother, with your folly, spoilt my play,
Marred our great rites, and placed a brand of shame
On your son's wife, and on our noble house,
Which were I chaste as Dian would not out.
 Aure. I hope thy story's true—upon my soul!
 First Priestess. I know her story's false—upon my soul!
If there's a wanton left in Rome, 'tis she!
 Pom. (*To First Priestess.*) Thou'lt never be a wanton!
  Wouldst know why?
No man in Rome would play at kisses with thee.
 Clo. A blind man might, Pompeia.
 Pom.   Not if he had
A nose!
 First Priestess. The curse of Dian on you both, you
  strumpets!
But here comes Cæsar, he will see through you.

   CÆSAR *enters with* ABRA *and attendants.*

 Cæs. What means this scene of wild confusion?   Peace!
As Rome's great Pontifex I must command it!
        (*Looks at* CLODIUS.)
Why Clodius, my friend, and is that thou?
(*Laughs.*) Is it a male or female costume, that
Which hangs so airily about thy limbs?
Art masquerading as a Vestal Virgin?
A better part thou surely couldst not play;
And yet a man's attire becomes thee better.
 Clo. Laugh on, great Cæsar.   As I've lost the game,
Of course I'll pay the forfeit.   Curse these cats,
They've nearly stripped me.   Please now cut this short.
Order things as thou wilt.   And yet one word—
Blame not thy wife, for she is innocent.
 Cæs. Of course my wife is innocent.   For she
Is Cæsar's wife, and thus could not be false.
And thou art Cæsar's friend, and could not be
A secret foe to Cæsar.   Let that pass.
But thou hast outraged all the women of Rome,
By thus profaning their most sacred rites
In honor of their goddess Bona Dea!
The Courts must judge what heavy penalty
Is meet for such a crime.

Clo.   That is all right.
(*Aside.*) Rome's Judges nowadays are ever for sale;
Just like so many steers within their stalls.
    Cæs. For thee, Pompeia, thou art innocent;
So Clodius says; and so full well I know.
But Cæsar's honored wife must ever be
Far more than that. Not only innocent;
She must not be suspected. Here I tear
Our marriage bond to pieces. (*Produces and tears bond.*)
                        Take her keys,
Aurelia, emblem of her wifely state.
Divorced I now declare thee.
    Pom.   Take your keys!
Now, Cæsar, you can marry meek Calpurnia;
Whom you love better than you e'er loved me.
    Cæs. To-morrow, so it please thee, fair Pompeia,
Depart for thine own home. Take with thee all
Thou brought'st to Cæsar, all that he has given.
Aurelia, see she goes in fitting state,
As one who once was Caius Cæsar's wife,
Within my chariot, guarded by my slaves,
Her purse well filled with gold.
Come, Clodius, now we will withdraw, my friend,
And let the sacred rites go peaceful on.

END OF ACT II.

ACT III.

THE PASSAGE OF THE RUBICON.

SCENE I.—*Night. Moonlight. Open country. The small
            river Rubicon.*

Enter CÆSAR, ANTONY, CORNELIUS *and* SOOTHSAYER.

    Cæs. 'Tis a sweet night. How quiet all things seem!
The moonlight sleeps upon the dreamy earth,
As if no tumult e'er could break its rest.
Oh, peaceful earth! oh, patient, meek-browed earth!
Sad mother of the whirlwind and the storm!
—Is that the Rubicon?

Cor.   It is, my lord.

Cæs. 'Tis a small stream to bound so great a world.
Is there a ford?

Cor.   The ford is just below.

Cæs. What is the hour?

Cor.   'Tis nearly midnight now.

Cæs. Still 'tis to-day then. And then comes to-morrow.
And after that, what then? Cornelius,
My heart is heavy—for I dreamed last night
A foul, unnatural dream.

Cor.   What was't, my lord?

Cæs. A dream that frights me yet. I dreamed I raised
This hand of mine in open, impious strife
Against my honored mother, who now dwells
Among the gods—if death does not end all.

Ant. Dreams are but phantoms, Cæsar, born of care
And the unruly mind. They are but fumes
Of bodily excess—of fevered brains—
And all which throws the system out of tune.
Thou art a sage, Cornelius; is it not
As I have said?

Cor.   Doubtless 'tis often thus.
Dreams oft are merely memories of the past,
Marred and confused.

Cæs.   Your words no doubt are true,
My worthy friends—and yet not all the truth.
The Mount of Wisdom lies halfway between
The gulfs of Unbelief and Superstition;
And I am well assured the immortal gods
Oft visit men in sleep, and mostly so
Those who are favorites; and with whose lives
The destinies of nations are inwove.
And thus my dream affrights me. Does it say,
Cross not the Rubicon; Rome is thy mother?

Cor. Thy mother would not seek to take thy life!
Thou dost not menace Rome, but those who tear
Our Rome to pieces with their crimes and lust.
Thou goest to save thy mother from the hands
Of those who would outrage her.

Ant.   It is truth.
Hast thou not offered them the hand of peace,
And have they not refused it with stern scorn?
Why was I forced to fly, save as thy friend,

Disguised, and in the night?   Go on to Rome,
Unguarded by thy legions,—and the fate
That Clodius met, that fate will soon be thine.
There is no choice.   Meet force with force, or die
At the proud feet of Pompey.   Then, perhaps,
Thy friends may save their lives by bending low
At Pompey's knees, and telling how they sinned
In loving Caius Cæsar.   But I have done.
   Sooth. In virtue of my office, I declare,
Great Cæsar, that thy dream has other purport
Than thou wouldst place upon it.   Rome, indeed,
Is thy great mother.   If within thy soul,
There lurks a thought to do that mother wrong,
By mean ambition, selfish lust of power,
Desire to wreak thy vengeance on her sons,
To be, in one short word, another Sylla,
Then cross not that small stream, but quick disband
Thy legions ; dying, if need be, a man.
But if thy aims be pure—if thou to Rome
Wilt be as a deliverer and restorer—
A champion of the poor, now trodden down
Beneath the feet of spoilers—and a foe
To all that now corrupts and harms the State—
Then go on boldly, and, in the great name
Of Jupiter the Mighty, I invoke
Upon thy head, the blessing of the gods!
           (*Outspreads his hands, as invoking blessing.*)
   Cæs. This deed once done can never be undone.
Think not I hesitate because I fear
Aught for myself—my thoughts are all of Rome!
I draw a sword now that I ne'er can sheathe,
Till I or Pompey master all the world.
Therefore I pause.   That little stream once passed,
The die is thrown!—We cannot take it back.
Oh, that the gods who feel for human woe,
Who love the right, and execrate the wrong,
Would stoop from high Olympus to make known
The course these feet should take.   Could I but know
Their sovereign will, at once would I obey,
Nor care if death and ruin were my doom.
—Ha! what is that?
(*An Apparition appears on the other side of the Rubicon,
   and beckons to him slowly.   It then disappears.*)
   2*

Didst see it, Antony ?
Arrayed with sword and shield like mighty Mars !
  Ant. In faith I did.   It seemed to beckon, " Come !"
  Sooth. It was a phantom sent by the great gods,
In answer to thy prayer.   It bade thee " Come !"
  Cæs. " Come?"   Yes, by Hercules !   Cornelius,
What dost thou say to that ?   It is the will
Of the immortal gods !   'Twere sacrilege
Longer to pause, when they have marked the way.
I doubt no longer.   All my path is clear,
As if my eyes could pierce this gloom to Rome.
Let us go on.   Led by triumphant Mars,
We cannot fail to scatter all our foes.
Our force as yet is small, but Cæsar's name
Will bring recruits by thousands.   Pompey says,
He need but stamp his foot upon the ground,
To raise an army.   I'll try stamping too ; ·
And see whose stamp is most effectual.

Enter a MESSENGER.

  Mess. My lord, your faithful Gaul sends me to say,
That it has raised some twenty cohorts for you.
  Cæs. (*Laughs.*) They hear my stamp in Gaul already
          then !

Enter another MESSENGER.

  2d Mess. Cæsar, I come from the army of Domitius.
The soldiers bade me say they would desert
His standard in a body, when you came
Within sight of their eagles.
  Cæs. Ha ! Antony ! they hear my stamp there too !
Aye, we will cross the Rubicon, and lead
Our swelling forces straightway into Rome.
Before wise Pompey wakes up from his sleep,
Our troops shall camp before the seven-hilled town.
I long to cross that stream, and break at once
With all my enemies.   And so they thought
I would disband my legions—bare my neck
To Pompey's sword, and yield up all my friends
To slaughter and to pillage?   By the gods,
What do they take me for ? -Or more, or less,
Than mortal man ?   Haply, they'll find me more.
Midnight is past ; and daylight lies before.
                          (*Exeunt all.*)

SCENE II.—*A Public Place in Rome.*

Enter CASSIUS *and* CICERO.

Cass. They scamper off like rats before the cat.
To-morrow there'll not be in all this Rome
A dozen Senators. What's Pompey doing?
Cic. He's still at Capua—so Brutus says.
Cass. Aye, *still* enough, I warrant. Where's his foot—
That foot whose stamp upon the ground he said
Would raise an army? Now he has the sword
That old Marcellus gave him with such pomp,
And bade him save the State, why does he stand
As if't would use itself? What does he mean—
To fly from Italy, and leave Rome bound
At Cæsar's footstool?
Cic.   It would seem so, truly.
Cass. Well, follow you the crowd? Or will you stay
And meekly bend the suppliant knee to Cæsar?
Cic. What do you say, my Cassius? Is it wise
To seek one's safety in a general wreck;
Or go down like a hero with the ship?
Cass. The ship will not go down—unless its crew
Desert their oars, and quail before the storm.
Shall we, the best of Rome, allow this Cæsar—
This creature of the mob, to beard the Senate,
Scoff at its orders, give up to the rabble
The public lands, divide the public treasure,
The spoils of war, among the common herd;
And strip the nobles as the Gracchi would
Had not their lives been shortened? Cicero,
Are you a Senator, and have a doubt
As to your duty?
Cic.   If we win, what then?
Cass. Imitate Sylla! Cut the foul weeds down.
He stopped too soon, or now we should have peace.
Ev'n when he pardoned Cæsar, he cried out,
" 'Tis weakness—for there's many a Marius
In that rebellious youth."
Cic.   Yes, either way,
Cæsar or Pompey, lies a path of blood.
Yet Pompey is my choice, as well you know—
As one it seems must rule. Alas, the reign

Of Law and Justice seems now dead in Rome.
But here comes Brutus.   Let us hear him first.

Enter BRUTUS.

Bru. Why do you linger here?   The rumor goes
That Cæsar's troops are closing in around us.
To-night I leave for Capua and Pompey.
    Cass. Has Cato gone?   He surely will not stay?
    Bru. My uncle Cato went some days ago
To Sicily, whose safe defence has been
Intrusted to his care.   'Tis a grave task.
    Cic. But thou art safe.   Thou hast no need to fly.
Cæsar's thy mother's friend ; and will be thine.
    Bru. But he is Cato's foe—and more, the foe
Of Rome and Freedom.   I can ne'er forget
I am a Brutus.   While a Brutus lives,
No king can reign in Rome.   So, it is said,
The oracle replied, when asked how long
Great Rome should flourish.   When do you go forth,
My worthy Cassius?

Enter SACULIA *and* CITIZENS.

    Sacu. Ah, here's a party of them.   Have you heard
That Cæsar's near at hand?   Ah, Cicero,
You are a trimmer, aren't you?   Pray, which side
Of the fence art sitting now, Cæsar's or Pompey's?
    Cic. Peace, babbler!   Learn to reverence the men
Whom the wise gods have fitly placed above thee.
To know one's place—that is a piece of wisdom
That ev'n a fool may have, and be no fool.
    Sacu. Hast on thy breastplate, Cicero?   The one
Thou worest in the Campus Martius,
When we poor voters were to be dismayed?
Put it on now—perhaps 'twill frighten Cæsar.
'Twould gladden Pompey's heart, to see that breastplate
Come shining down the road to Capua!
He'd know the battle was half won already.
    Cic. Saculia, thou wert better far employed
In mending rents in togas, than in making
Sad rents in the fair state.   Go, get thy needle!
And I'll give thee a job.   My robe is torn.
    Sacu. And thou, smooth Cicero, wert better employed
In pettifogging out the eyes of Justice,

To save some guilty knave, than hatching plots
With two such traitors as these!
    Cass.   Traitors, you scum!
Go to your cobbling, to your mending of soles!
    First Cit. I'm not a cobbler—but I can cobble you.
                             (Menaces Cassius.)
    Sec. Cit. I'm not a mender of bad soles, young Brutus;
But I can mend your soul, and manners too.
                           (Menaces Brutus.)
    Sacu. (*Interfering.*) Come, come, good citizens, this would
        not please
Great Cæsar. For he wishes no disturbance.
Go on your way, proud sirs—there may be those
Not far behind, more difficult to manage.
    Cass. Come, Brutus, let's get out of this cursed rat-hole.
We'll come back soon, each bearing a good whip.
Come, Cicero! you see they need a master.
              (Exeunt CASSIUS, BRUTUS *and* CICERO.)
    Sacu. (*Calls after them.*) You are near-sighted, Cassius—
        better take
Cicero's arm—he'll keep you out of rat-holes.
Cicero, how much are vetches nowadays?
Your father was a gardener, I've heard,
And famous for his vetches. So they called
Him Cicero! Brutus, your worthy father
Was a Plebeian, and no more descended
From the great Junius Brutus, than I am
A son of Hercules. A curse on them!
Talk of their blood! The best they have is stolen
From us Plebeians, and the rest's as thin
And weak and watery as milk that's skimmed
Three mornings over. "Blue"—of course it's blue,
From so much skimming.
    First Cit. As for that Brutus, he's not even the son
Of his own father—so the gossips say.
    Sec. Cit. Whose son is Brutus then?
    First Cit.   Why, he's his—mother's.
    Sacu. That much is mostly certain. You have heard
The story too? I'd think so, if his heart
Were softer, and he loved the people more.
Come, let us on unto the Forum. Cæsar
May be in Rome at any moment now.   *(Exeunt.)*

SCENE III.—*The Forum in Rome.*

Enter SEXTUS, *followed by* CHRYSOGONUS.

Chry. Dost think, brave Sextus, that Cæsar is near at hand?

Sex. He moves like lightning. He may be now at the gates of Rome, for all I know. Then comes our turn again. I wouldn't give a pea-pod for the heads of those who waylaid and murdered my dear Clodius.

Chry. Thou knowest I had nothing to do with that, Sextus.

Sex. I know thou sayest so.

Chry. I swear to thee I had not, Sextus. I might have seemed to dislike him—but it was all seeming. If there was a man I admired in Rome, it was Clodius. Such manners! Such an example to all the young men! Nobody could toss off a goblet of wine as he could.

Sex. No! nor wink at a woman. Ah, he's gone—and left no equal behind him.

Chry. Dost think it safe for me to stay in Rome, now Cæsar is in power?

Sex. Of course it is. Stay by all means.

Chry. But he said he would not spare me—if ever he got the upper hand.

Sex. Words! words! what does an eagle care for a caterpillar? He will not even recognise thee when he sees thee.

Chry. I think so too. Yes, I will stay. Thank thee, Sextus, for thy good counsel.

Sex. (*Aside.*) The villain! Cæsar will know him at a glance. And punish him for that Roscius affair, and a dozen other murders.

Enter CASSIUS, BRUTUS *and* CICERO.

Cass. (*Goes to Sextus.*) Is there late news from Cæsar?
   Tell me, Sextus.

Sex. Cassius, thou didst me once a kindness. Hear! Cæsar may be in Rome within an hour.

Cass. Is't really so?

Sex.   True as thou art alive.

Cass. (*To Cicero and Brutus.*) The tiger's at the gate.

Cic. What meanest thou?

Cass. Cæsar's at hand. We have no time to lose.
Wilt thou go, Cicero; or wilt thou stay?

Thou hast thy choice, but no one can do both.
Thou art too great a man to be allowed
To take no side, but wait the side that wins.
Thou stayest here—then thou art Cæsar's friend,
And Pompey's enemy. Thou goest with us;
Then art thou Cæsar's foe, and Pompey's friend.
Make up thy mind—thou hast no time to lose.
Come, Brutus; we will leave the Southern gate,
Cæsar will enter from the North. Farewell,
My Cicero. We'll say we left thee halting,
Just like the ass in the old fable, 'twixt
The rival stacks of hay.
    Bru.   Before we reach
The Southern gate, thou'lt surely glad our hearts
By joining us, good Cicero. For thou hast
Too great a name to fling it like a pearl
Into the mire beneath a tyrant's feet.
Thou owest a debt to coming centuries, friend.
Such men as thou should live not for one age,
But all the ages.
    Cic.   Brutus, thou art right.
I'll hesitate no longer. Where the best
Of Rome's sons gather, is the place for me.
If Rome can yet be saved, Pompey's the man.
We all remember how he met the foe
When Mithridates, hot child of the sun,
Streamed forth from Pontus o'er Bithynia,
And on our Asia laid his conquering arm.
But we must hasten, for this Cæsar moves
As on the wings o' the wind. Let us to Pompey—
And then to Greece, to Asia—where he will.
Where we are is the Senate, and where that,
Were it the depths of Afric, there is Rome!
           (*Exeunt, R.,* BRUTUS, CASSIUS *and* CICERO.)
           Enter, L., SACULIA *and* CITIZENS.
    Sacu. Ha, Sextus; what's the latest news from Cæsar?
    Sex. Cæsar is near at hand. See how the nobles,
Those heroes of the fish-ponds, fly in fear
At sound of Cæsar's tread. 'Tis well they haste—
His speed is like the lightning's.
    Sacu.   Yes, and when
The lightning strikes, why then we shall hear thunder.

(*Points to Chry.*) What does that knave do here? 'Twould
                    serve him right,
To send him to join Roscius.
 Sex.   Peaceful now.
Leave him to Cæsar. Cæsar saw it all ;
And he has a long memory.

     A flourish of trumpets without.

 Sex.   Here he comes—
Like Mars or Jupiter ! Hurra for Cæsar !
 Sacu. Old bull-neck's coming ! Hurra, my boys, 'tis
   Cæsar!
 Cits. Hurra for Cæsar !
 Chry.   Hurra for Cæsar !

Amid the cheering, enter CÆSAR, ANTONY, CORNELIUS *and*
     Soldiers.

 Cæs. Thanks, my good friends ! Your welcome back to
   Rome
Is sweet to me, as to the mariner,
Who long has buffeted the angry waves,
The sight of land and home. Ah, my good Sextus,
The sight of thee is pleasant. Clodius I heard,
Was slain by villains.
 Sex.   Welcome, mighty Cæsar !
Hadst thou been here, my Clodius had not died
By traitors' hands, because he loved the people.
 Chry. Welcome, great Cæsar ! Say but thou the word,
We'll take revenge on Clodius' murderers.
Tear down their houses—spoil and burn and slay ;
As Sylla did when he was uppermost.
 Cæs. And who art thou that giv'st such fiery counsel ?
 Chry. Chrysogonus, my lord ; who once belonged
To savage Sylla. But the kindly gods
Have shown me how I erred ; and now I swear
To live and die by Cæsar and the people.
 Cæs. It is well sworn, Chrysogonus—for thou
Shalt surely die by Cæsar and the people.
Thy hands are crimson with the blood of Roscius.
Dost thou remember what I promised thee,
If ever power were mine ? Swords here, my guards !

   Two soldiers step forward with bared swords.
Seize ye that villain ! No, profane not steel

With his base blood.   Take him and hurl the wretch
From the Tarpeian rock ; that Rome may know
That Justice reigns once more within her walls.
    Chry. Mercy, great Cæsar !   Mercy !
    Cæs.   Mercy for thee
Were cruelty to Rome.   Off with him, men !
                   (*Guards drag off* CHRYSOGONUS.)
That ends the list of my proscriptions, Romans.
Shall we who hated Sylla tread his path ?
I have not come to Rome to slay, my friends.
I've come to heal and pacify the State.
Who strikes a needless blow does Cæsar wrong.
I hear that Rome's deserted of the nobles,
Flying in fear.   Would they had stayed to learn
From Cæsar's lips how kind his purpose is.
(*To Sextus.*) Has Cato gone ?
    Sex.   He fled a week ago.
    Cæs. And Cicero ?   He knows I love him well ;
My old schoolfellow.   Does he also fly,
As if I were a Fury ?
    Sex.   Till to-day
He seemed to hesitate ; but then he went.
Brutus persuaded him.   They went together ;
Along with Cassius.
    Cæs. (*Agitated.*) What, Brutus gone !
Why, Pompey killed his father !   It must be false.
Brutus would surely stay, and learn of me
What are my plans.
    Sex.   He's set his life of late
After the mould of Cato's.
    Cæs.   Foolish boy !
Cato's a dreamer !   For he talks and acts
As if we lived in Plato's feigned Republic,
Instead of this most complex one of Rome.
Some men, my Antony, are like fair fields,
Which oft grow weeds in sheer luxuriance,
But also grow rich grains.   While other men
Are narrow, dry and sterile, like a cave,
Which bears no weeds, but also bears no fruit.
And Cato is a cave.—When did they leave ?
    Sex. Not half an hour ago they all were here.
They soon could be o'ertaken and brought back,
They have so little vantage.

Cæs.   Antony!
Take horse and overtake them.   Bring them back!
  Ant. Cæsar, I will.   Dead or alive, I'll bring them.
  Cæs. No, harm them not.   If Brutus will not come,
Why, let him go.   Mind that thou harm him not!
Upon thy life I charge thee!
  Ant.   Fear not me;
I'll be as tender with him as his nurse.   *(Starts to go.)*
  Cæs. On second thought, we'll let them go in peace,
And so they will, my Antony.   Let them go!
They will be wiser men when they come back.
  Ant. So be it, Cæsar.   *(Aside.)* Cæsar is afraid
To trust his darling Brutus in my hand,
Lest I should squeeze too hard.   And so I would,
By Bacchus!

Enter a MESSENGER.

  Mess. Cæsar, I bring thee word from Capua.
Pompey has sailed for Greece—perhaps for Asia.
He bade me say he would not talk with thee,
Save with his sword, upon the fateful field.
He bids thee to dismiss thy numerous legions,
Obey the Senate, come to him in Greece;
And then he'll use his powerful influence
To see that thou'rt forgiven.
  Cæs.   Was Pompey sober,
And in sane mind, when thus he talked with thee?
  Mess. He seemed so, Cæsar.
  Cæs.   Whom the angry gods
Wish to destroy, they first make proud and mad.
He might learn that in Greece, Cornelius.
Well, we will follow him to Macedon,
To Asia, Afric, wheresoe'er he goes.
He will not meet us?   We will then meet him.
He thinks to play great Sylla's cunning game;
O'erwhelming Rome with all the mighty East.
We'll break that thunder-cloud before 'tis formed.
Antony, tell my legions that their march
Is just begun.   We start at once to seek
This braggart foe in Macedonia.
  (To Cits.) All ye who wish to further Cæsar's cause,
Can find a place beneath his conquering eagles.
His soldiers are his children.   All the spoils

Of war he shares with them.   Ask and you'll learn
This is no idle boast, but simple truth.—
Come, Antony; if Pompey will have war,
We'll test which of us has the mightier star !
(Exeunt all.)

END OF ACT III.

ACT IV.

AFTER PHARSALIA.

SCENE I.—*A Street in Rome.*

Enter SACULIA *and* CITIZENS.

First Cit. And were you in the battle, Saculia ?

Sacu. By the sword of Mars you might think so.   You know that when Cæsar invited us citizens to fill up his ranks, as I was an old soldier, I could do no other than join him.

Sec. Cit. Fun—wasn't it ?

Sacu. Why ye-es, fighting's prodigious fun !   That is— so long as you are chasing the other fellows.   But, it becomes rather too exciting when the other fellows turn, and begin to chase you.

First Cit. But how of the battle ?   Tell us all about it.

Sacu. Well, it was at a place called Pharsalia.   Pompey had more than twice as many men as we had ; but then, you know, we were veterans.   I didn't see everything, not being able, like many old soldiers, to be in all parts of the field at the same time.   Therefore I can only tell you what I saw myself, and what others told me.   Cæsar didn't consult me about the plan of the battle at all !

First Cit. Didn't their cavalry scare you when they came thundering down ?

Sacu. Yes ; for they were seven thousand to our one thousand.   But Cæsar—he's a shrewd one, I tell you—had trained a lot of us foot soldiers to act with the cavalry, and told us just what to do.   'Twas a good idea, by Hercules ! (*Laughs.*)

Sec. Cit. How was it ?

Sacu. Why, you see, all the good-looking young nobles of Rome were in their cavalry ; and Cæsar told us to push our javelins at their eyes and faces—as they would hate having their beauty spoiled more than they would being killed. And so we did. And, after a little while of that kind of thing, they swore we were cowards, and were afraid to fight fair; and turned tail, the whole posse of them, and ran for their lives—no, for their good looks.

First Cit. Nobody but Cæsar would have thought of that.

Sacu. No—for he knows how it is himself—he is a famous lady's man, you know.

Sec. Cit. And they say their tents were splendid !

Sacu. Oh, magnificent—ivy and roses trained over them, and all that sort of thing. Silver dishes and gold goblets too! And their slaves had everything ready for a fine dinner, by the time they should come back, all tired from thrashing Cæsar. Poor fellows! fifteen thousand lay dead on the field—and twenty-five thousand surrendered next morning.

First Cit. And Cæsar pardoned all of them ?

Sacu. He pardoned the whole of them—Senators, nobles and all. If Pompey had not run off, I believe he would have pardoned him too. Ah, well, it was better that the Egyptians should cut his head off, than that Cæsar should pardon him.

First Cit. Yes—he'd only be making fresh trouble.

Sacu. And his head was getting to be worth very little to any one—though I suppose he didn't want to part with it.

First Cit. I suppose not. We all have our little weaknesses. And Pompey always had an obstinate disposition.

Sec. Cit. Yes, some men have—especially old men.

Sacu. Yes, yes—very few old men are willing to die when their time comes, and their heirs begin to wish them out of the way. Man is an obstinate animal—just as bad as a mule. Poor, weak human nature!

First Cit. Let's go up to the Forum, and see what's going on to-day. Perhaps Cæsar will be there.

Sacu. As you say, friends. My share of the spoils, will make me a man of leisure for many a day.

(*Exeunt omnes.*)

Scene II.—*A Public Place in Rome.*

Enter Cicero *and* Cassius.

Cic. Well, you must own in fairness, Cassius,
That Cæsar's clemency o'ertops the height
Of aught e'er seen in Rome.   For me, I feared
A second Marius.   But he is bland
And soft as summer.   Not a word is breathed
Of bloody vengeance.   All his thoughts seem bent
To make of us, his enemies, firm friends.
   Cass. 'Twas a shrewd game, I grant.
   Cic.   'Tis more than shrewd,
My Cassius.   'Tis wise, and great, and good!
   Cass. Stuff! stuff!   Why did he save us?   'Twas to bring
Us home to Rome like captives, bound with bonds
Invisible, but stroug as iron bands.
We simply grace his triumph—just the same
As if we followed at his chariot wheels,
Our limbs bent down 'neath chains.   We serve him better,
Thus witnessing his glory and our shame,
Than if we lay, all mouldering, stiff and cold,
On sad Pharsalia's field.
   Cic.   We played our game,
And we have lost it.   Had we won, his life,
And that of all his friends, had been the forfeit.
He wins, and yet he spares.   Takes no man's land,
Degrades no man.   Would we have done the same,
Had we been conquerors?   You know we would not.
   Cass. Of course we would not.   Sylla was wiser far
Than Cæsar e'er will be ;—and he ne'er spared
A foe, or e'er forsook a friend.   Mark this!
Cæsar's a fool!
   Cic.   Better to be a fool,
A generous fool, than be a cruel god!
But as for Cæsar, he is greater far
Than ever Sylla was.   Wisely to speak,
Is to be great.   To write with Cæsar's pen,
Is to be greater still.   To act, still greater.
He then who cau do all—speak, write and act—
And of them all is master, is a mau
Whose claim to be called great, must be allowed
Against both hate and envy.   That's my mind.

Cass. Oh, if a man can *act*—and make a sure,
Deep mark with his good sword—it is enough
To stamp him great with me.   As for the pen,
And the glib tongue, we're better off without them.
But mark my words—for time will prove them true.
Cæsar's a fool!   Only a fool would think
He could mix oil and water.   There's too much hate
'Tween him and us, to live in peace together.
      Cic. What then?—another war?
      Cass.   War was a blunder!
There are more ways than war for men to die.
                    (*Cicero manifests alarm.*)
Enough of this.   These are but idle thoughts,
My Cicero;—thrown out in random mood,
More than for thought of action.
      Cic.   So I trust.
But even thoughts like those are dangerous.
Please keep all such, my friend, for other ears.
I am too old for a conspirator.
      Cass. Of course—of course—'twas a mere argument,
Having no meaning, save an idle mood.
You've written much the same to Atticus.
      Cic. (*Alarmed.*) Not I.   Indeed, indeed, you miscon-
                    strue.
      Cass. Tut!   I will not betray you.   We are all
In the same boat, we Senators of Rome.
      Cic. Let a man make a hundred wise remarks,
They'll be forgotten.   Let him breathe but once
A piece of folly, straightway it is told
All over Rome.
      Cass.   Of course it is.   And why?
Because a thistle is the food of asses.
They always treat me so—then why not you?
But, by the way, what do you think, my friend,
Of the new Senators?   There is some more
Of our great Cæsar's doings.
      Cic.   Oh, 'tis horrible!
To thrust barbarians 'mong the Conscript Fathers.
Perhaps you saw that lusty giant from Gaul?
      Cass. Of course!   Next we shall have some savage chief
From Britain's isle—naked, with painted skin!
You know they have their wives in common there.
But that's not unlike Rome.

Cic.   No, more's the pity!
Ah, these are solemn times! No virtue's left—
No reverence for rank, or birth, or mind.
All will be buried 'neath a muddy flow
Of dirty waters, raked up from below.

Enter BRUTUS.

Cass. Good morrow, Brutus!
Bru.   Health to you, my Cassius!
And you, my Cicero! What's the news to-day?
Cass. Oh, nothing! only we shall have a king
In Rome within the year.
Bru.   No, Cassius!
Cass.   Why,
We have a king already, save in name.
Where the thing is, the name will follow soon.
Bru. Cæsar will never dare a step like that.
Cass. Perhaps not. But last night some unknown hand
Placed crowns of laurel upon all his statues.
Cic. Ha! That is growing bold indeed. What wretch,
My noble Brutus, could have moved in this?
Bru. It is enough to make the mighty soul
Of Junius Brutus come back from the shades.
Cass. (*Aside.*) I thought that scheme would work. Say
                    the word king,
And Rome will tremble to its Capitol.
Call the king Consul, Emperor, Dictator,
And then it is all smooth. But men are fools!
Cic. What is it that you mutter, Cassius?
Cass. Oh, nothing.
Bru.   Cassius seems not pleased to-day.
Cic. Oh, were he pleased—why then he would not be
Old Caius Cassius.
Cass.   Thank you, Cicero.
But you're a lawyer, that's a falsifier.
Were lawyer's swords as sharp as are their tongues,
They'd cut the world in slices, and divide
It up among them, like a stolen orange.
Bru. (*Laughs.*) You're even now, I think. Come now
                    with me.
I go to call on Cæsar at his palace.
'Tis his reception hour, when all may go.
He will be glad to see us, for he bade
Me come whene'er I could, and bring my friends.

Cass. Well, we'll go too. (*Aside.*) Cæsar's as kind to
       Brutus
As most men to their sons.—Come, Cicero!
Cæsar admires your genius, as he calls it.

SCENE III.—*Room in* CÆSAR'S *Palace, as before.*

Enter CÆSAR *and* CORNELIUS.

Cæs. I'm weary! weary! good Cornelius.
I'm tired, and sick at heart. Time.is at best
But like a flight of stairs; which falls away
Behind us, thundering down in the abyss,
As fast as we ascend. And thus to stay
All idly where we are, is but to fall.
To mount forever is life. While still the prize
Was to be won, I nerved me to the task.
But now my foes are conquered, justice done
To me and to my friends, and Rome at peace,
I feel that Cæsar could lie down and die.
     Cor. 'Tis the recoil of many wearing years
Of active, dangerous strife. Your weary marches
Iu Gaul and Germany—your late campaigns
In Macedon and Spain. Such active toil
In marching, fighting, planning, with your life
Always in peril—all your nerves strung up
To the high pitch—must needs result at last
In utter weariness. Give yourself rest,
Retire as much as may be from the crowd,
Take all things easy for a few short years,
And you shall find Cæsar is young again.
     Cæs. Dost know, Cornelius, I have sometimes thought
Of doing even as old Sylla did?
Give up all offices, resign all power,
Become a simple citizen of Rome,
Retire to some sweet villa on the coast,
And with my books and pen enjoy my life.
I look out on the world, and all seems dark,
Fierce and tempestuous, as a stormy sky
In a wild night. But then I see sweet homes,
Like peaceful spots of blue amid the gloom,
And little children shining there like stars.
Were not that better far than all this strife?

Cor. True, Cæsar, I myself have always thought
That happiness lay not in wealth or power,
But in the golden mean 'tween high and low.
The wheel of Fortune speeds along its way;
Those at the top move fastest—so their hour
Is o'er the sooner. And along the ground
The wheel moves slow, with a perpetual grind.
Give me the centre of the wheel—there glides
Our still life onward, free of chance or change.
But great men cannot dwell there, much I fear.
What would thy friends say?—what Calpurnia?
And couldst thou do it, and live?

Cæs. Oh, as to life,
That would not matter much. A few short years,
And death will claim us all. And after that,
What then? I thought at one time with Lucretius,
That, formed from out dull atoms, we at the end,
To atoms should return. But can this soul,
That burns so brightly in its earthly lamp,
Go out in death, and cease to be, and die?
My mother—noble, good Aurelia!
My daughter Julia—so loving and true!
Can their pure souls have vanished like a flame
Blown out by the mad wind? It cannot be.
I feel within me that it cannot be.
But call Calpurnia, kind Cornelius.
I wish to talk with her.   (*Exit* CORNELIUS.)
And is there one that loves great Cæsar for
Himself alone—now that Aurelia's dead?
My mother—she I knew was truth itself;
But who now can I trust?

Enter CALPURNIA.

Calpurnia!

Cal. Cæsar! My lord!
Cæs.   I've had a thought, Calpurnia.
Thou art, my wife, the first of women in Rome.
Cal. Thanks to thee, Cæsar! But do I not wear
My honors as becomes great Julius' wife?
I've sought to do so, but perchance I've failed.
Still I am apt to learn. What shall I do
To show that Cæsar's wife is worthy Cæsar?
Cæs. Cæsar can find no fault with Cæsar's wife.

3

She wears her honors as a rose its red.
Calpuruia!
 Cal. Well, my lord.
 Cæs.   I had a dream—
A silly dream; but I will tell it thee.
How wouldst thou like to lay thy honors down?
How wouldst thou like that I should put aside
All shows and pomps of power as Sylla did—
All high commands, all offices of state—
And be a simple citizen of Rome?
Go to some villa by the murmuring sea;
And there we two should live and love until
Death came at last with his consuming fire.
What say'st. Calpurnia—would this please thee, sweet?
 Cal. Oh, Cæsar—oh, my husband! could this be,
It were a gift of the immortal gods!
I live in constant terror now, my Cæsar;
Not for myself, but thee. What is this state,
Beneath a sword, just hanging by a hair?
The nobles dread thee, Cæsar. All thy love
Returns on thee in hatred. This I see
With my keen woman's eye—because my sight
Is sharpened by my love. Oh, let us fly
From this accurséd Rome, which reeks with blood,
And live for one another—not for men
Who cannot feel or love or gratitude,
And in return for honors give but hate.

   Enter a Slave, and hands letter to CALPURNIA.

 Slave. A letter for my lord.   (*Exit Slave.*)
 Cal. (*Smiles.*) It is a woman's writing, Julius.
 Cæs. (*Takes letter.*) 'Tis from Servilia. She agrees with
       thee.
      (*Hands letter to Calpurnia.*)
 Cal. (*Reads.*) "Guard thyself, Cæsar. All the nobles
      hate thee.
Cicero, Casca, Cassius—even, oh,
That I should have to say it, my own son,
My Brutus! For he says thou mean'st to make
Thyself a king. And also keep thy eye
On Decimus. From thy old friend,
      Servilia."
 Cæs. (*Gloomily.*) Cicero, Cassius, Casca! All their lives

Were mine, by doom of war.   I hailed them friends,
And raised them from their humble, suppliant knees.
I touched not their estates, levied no fines,
But gave them a full pardon.   Brutus, too!
I gave strict orders he should not be harmed
Upon the day of battle.   They have sworn
Unto the gods, as all the Senate have sworn,
Perdition to the wretch who touched my life.
When men scorn oaths, how then can they be held?
They keep no terms—how then can I keep terms?
There's only one safe course with men like these.

    Cal. And what is that?

    Cæs.   The unsparing sword of Sylla!

    Cal. Oh no, my husband.   Let not loose again
The vengeful sword of Sylla.   Surely these men,
The chief of Rome, have souls that can be touched.
Kill them with kindness!   Pierce them to the heart
With favors past desert.   Make thus thy cause
Their cause, and turn these enemies to friends.

    Cæs. It is a woman's counsel—but the gods
Perchance may smile upon it.   Well I know
There is no safety now, no sure repose
Save in the sword.   That would make certainty!
And yet I cannot do it—cannot give
Rome up again to vengeance.   Let death come
To me, if so it will.   For I am tired,
Calpurnia, of this unthankful task
Of striving to make whole a rotten State;
Whose noblest souls are dead to gratitude,
And think no more of breaking solemn oaths,
Than spilling a cup of wine.   But 'tis the hour
When I give audience.   Let the doors be opened.

    Cal. I will, my lord.   Great Pallas prosper thee,
And aid thee with her counsels.   (*Exit* CALPURNIA.)

Enter BRUTUS, CASSIUS, CICERO, ANTONY *and* DECIMUS.

    Bru. Hail, Cæsar!   Health and happiness attend thee!

    Cæs. And health and happiness to thee, my Brutus!
And to thee also, Cassius!   Cicero,
Thou'rt looking better.   Decimus, my friend!
Antony, thou art flourishing as usual,—
My strong right arm art thou!   What is the news
In Rome to-day?

Bru.   There is no news, I think;
Save of the rising of the Parthians.

Cæs. Yes, much I fear that I shall have to take
An army into Asia.   While I'm gone,
I'll need your help, my friends, both there and here.
I have been planning for the provinces.
You, Cassius, did good work in Syria,
When Parthia's mail-clad horsemen, swarming west,
Impinged against our power, and Crassus fell
Before the fierce Orodes.   Hapless man!
His head was severed from its bleeding trunk,
And in his mouth was poured the molten gold;
Orodes crying: "Take thou now thy fill
Of that which thou through life hast coveted!"
We need a man in Syria—one of steel!
How will that wealthy province meet thy views,
My worthy Cassius?

Cass.   Cæsar doth o'erpay
My poor deserts.   I am his servant ever.

Cæs. Brutus, my friend, thou hast done well in Gaul
Thou too shalt have a Province.   Macedon
Will suit thee well.   I know thou'lt govern wisely.

Bru. Cæsar, my thanks!   I'll strive to do my duty,
Alike to Macedonia and Rome.

Cæs. Brave Decimus, most faithful and most true
Cæsar has always found thee.   Thou hast been
Near to my side through many a long campaign.
I give to thee near Gaul.   They love me there,
And will receive thee gladly in my name.

Dec. As I have been, oh Cæsar, will I be—
Faithful and true, forever!   Many thanks!

Cæs. Thou, Cicero, I will not take from Rome.
Thy son-in-law I've named for Consul.   But
Thy place is in the Senate.   He wrongs Rome,
And wrongs the Senate, who would take the flower
And choicest ornament of these dull times,
The master orator of all the world,
And place him where his matchless speech could have
No fitting theme nor audience.   Cicero,
Thy name itself outranks all other titles.

Cic. Such praise from Cæsar makes all other honors
Seem mean and stale.   I'll strive henceforth to make
My poor orations worthy of his praise.

Cæs. The Senate, Brutus—does it meet to-day?

Bru. Yes, Cæsar; and I think the hour is near.
Had we not better leave, my friends?

Cic.   I think so.

Cæs. One moment. I am debtor to the Senate
For a long list of favours. Honor on honor
They heap upon me. I would not seem graceless;
Yet I could wish they now would let me pass.
I have a surfeit now of praise, my friends.
Please then think more of Rome, and less of me,
And you will please me better. Pardon me;
I would not seem discourteous—only Rome
Is suffering so for greatly needed laws,
To make its people prosperous and free.

Bru. (*Aside to Cass.*) That has a good ring, Cassius.

Cass. (*Aside.*) Pshaw, that's mere talk. Mere honey to
                        catch flies.

Cic. We'll try to meet your modest wishes, Cæsar.
But we are few, you know; and the great tide
Of gratitude to Cæsar, bears us on,
Despite our small obstruction.

Cæs.   Do your best,
And it will serve me.   .

(*Exeunt* BRUTUS, CASSIUS, CICERO *and* DECIMUS.)

Ant. A precious lot of scoundrels! Dost thou know
That scarce a man of the whole Senate is true?
And yet thou giv'st their leaders Prætorships,
And Provinces! By Jove, 'twere wiser far
To give me orders to take all their heads,
And hang them 'round the Forum. Give the word,
And I will do it too!

Cæs.   That's the sure course;
I know it well as thou. And yet, and yet,
I will not do it. No, my Antony,
Not even to save my life.

Ant.   Nor my life too?
The lives of all thy friends? What madness is this?
I've known thee in Gaul, to take ten thousand lives,
So it were necessary. And now thou haltest
At some half hundred, which would give us peace.

Cæs. They were barbarians. These are my brothers—
The noblest souls of Rome.

Ant.   Jove pity Rome,
If such men be her noblest. Thou hast given
Them all their lives—and now they menace thine.
Thou giv'st them cities, provinces, and still
'Twill be the same ; they'll kill thee if they can.
Trust thou a tiger—ask him not to tear
The hand that gives him food—but trust not thou
To one great lord in Rome. Thou lov'st the people.
That is enough for them ; outweighs all virtues,
Makes all agreements naught, and marks thee out
To die by open or by secret war,
As died the glorious Gracchi !
 Cæs.   Be it so !
Rome's had enough of blood. The world shall judge,
In after ages, 'tween their deeds and mine.
 Ant. "The world shall judge!" Cæsar, thy enemies
Are keepers of the record. They will taint
Thy glorious name to all succeeding time.
They make the histories. Thou hast no voice.
And all the coming ages 'll call thee tyrant !
 Cæs. Then I appeal to the great gods above!
They'll do me justice. Even on this earth,
Wrong cannot triumph ever. The great mass
Of mortal men will not lie always thus
Beneath the feet of proud and selfish nobles.
Freedom at last shall reign, if not in Rome,
Then in some new Atlantis of the West,
Beyond the mighty gate and boundless sea.
When that time comes, the world's heart shall begin
To know me as I am, a man who loved
And labored for the People !
 Ant.   Well—so be it !
If the worst comes, I'll die, my lord, with thee ;
Or, if I live, avenge thee! That curs'd Senate.
Thou mark'st their cunning and perfidious game?
 Cæs. I mark it well. It is to make me odious
To all the people. Make me seem ambitious,
Greedy for power and praise, beyond all men
That ever ruled in Rome. They'd smother me
'Neath flowers and peacock's feathers.
 Ant.   Mark that move
To place thy statue in the Capitol,
Among the kings of Rome—as if thou meant
To make thyself a king.

Cæs.   We'll block that game
This very day; according to the plan
We late arranged.   Hast thou prepared the crown?
   Ant. The crown is ready.   Wilt thou walk to-day?
   Cæs. In half an hour.
   Ant.   All shall be ready, Cæsar.
   Cæs. What folly, senseless folly, 'twere in me,
Having the substance, like the dog in the fable,
To risk it for a shadow, a mere shadow,
A name, an empty title!   Have they not,
This gracious Senate, showered upon my head
Titles enough?   Dictator, Emperor,
Commander of the Army, for my life!
More power than ever King was given in Rome.
What need I more?   To take the name of King
Would be to shock the people, now my friends,
And make them doubt my loyalty and truth.
I am too old a soldier, Antony,
To walk into this trap the Senate sets.

Enter CORNELIUS *hastily.*

   Cor. Cæsar, the Senate have just now resolved,
To give thee further honors, as they term them.
They've voted thou'rt not mortal, but a God!
That a new temple shall be built to thee,
As to great Romulus, and Antony here,
Shall be the Priest of the temple!
   Ant. (*Laughs.*)   I a Priest!
I'd like to offer them up on the altar,
As the first sacrifice to Cæsar's fame.
   Cor. A delegation from the Senate, now
Is on its way to bring thee news of this.
I hurried first, that thou might'st be prepared.

(CÆSAR *takes a seat.*)

   Cæs. (*Laughs.*) And so I am a God now! Well, I'll act
The god a little, and see how they like it.
A god!—I never felt so like a man
As I have felt this month past.   Oh, my friends,
Cæsar has won the world, and finds at last
It is not worth the winning.
   Cor.   Here they come!

Ant. I will go, Cæsar, to prepare our plans.

(*Exit* ANTONY.)

Enter Deputation of SENATORS.

Senator. Cæsar, we bring thee greetings from the Senate.

CÆSAR *remains silent and seated, gazing vacantly into the air.*

Sen. I say we bring thee greetings from the Senate.

CÆSAR *makes no response—takes no notice of them.*

Sen. (*Angrily.*) It ever has been the custom in our Rome
For citizens to rise, whene'er the Senate
Has deigned to honor them with Deputies.

Cæs. Oh yes, for citizens! But I'm a god,
By your own showing. Gods do never rise
When mortal men approach. Be I a god?
Then down upon your knees, and give your message.

Sen. Cæsar, so great an insult to the Senate,
Bars out all further words. We will report
To those who sent us, with what gross contempt
Their envoys were received.

Cæs. (*Rises.*)   Pray tell them this:—
Cæsar is not a god; but a mere man,
Who has found favor in his country's eyes.
The Senate would not like him as a god,
More than poor Cæsar thus would like himself.
If he were god, why then upon their knees
Should they approach him—which he would abhor
Ev'n more than they would. Would the Senate seek
To honor Cæsar further?—let them pass
The laws he has proposed to prosper Rome.
To set the poor at work, by draining all
The Pontine marshes and the Fucine lake.
By sending eighty thousand landless poor
To build up Carthage. Let them further pass
The law to give the Provinces a stake
In the Republic; making Senators
Of all their worthiest men, from Spain and Gaul
To Macedon and the far Syrian shore.
For thus we bind all in one equal bond.
All noble souls are kindred. Through the bars
Of country and of race they clasp warm hands.

And even o'er the yawning chasms wide
Of intervening centuries, they send
Their messages of warning and of cheer.
Thus honoring all, we build up the fair state
In still securer power; while all mankind
Shall hail a mother in almighty Rome!

Sen. Cæsar, we'll bear thy answer to the Senate.

Cæs. So do, and you will please me.

(*Exeunt* SENATORS.)

Cæs. (*To Cor.*)   Now for the games.

(*Exeunt* CÆSAR *and* CORNELIUS.)

SCENE IV.—*A Public Place in Rome.*

Enter SACULIA *and* CITIZENS.

Sacu. We are in good time. Something's going on to-day that'll be worth seeing, my masters. If it isn't so, call me screw-eye.

First Cit. What is it, Saculia?

Sacu. Never you mind; you'll see. Old Cæsar 'll show the people what he means. He'll stop here as he goes to the games.

First Cit. They say that Brutus says Cæsar wants to be king.

Sec. Cit. Well, if we had to have a king, Cæsar would be the man for me.

Sacu. We don't want a king. Cæsar wouldn't be a king. Brutus is a prig—he's got a nose of wax ; and his brother-in-law, old Cassius, squeezes it into just what shape he pleases.

First Cit. Here they are.

Sacu. Shout for Cæsar when he comes. Split your throats, boys!

Enter CÆSAR, CORNELIUS *and attendants.*

Sacu. and Cits. Hurra for Cæsar! Hurra!

Cæs. Thanks, my good friends. Cornelius, I will rest
Here a few moments. I feel weak to-day.

Cor. Here is the chair of state the Senators
Have placed for thee.

(CÆSAR *takes seat in golden chair.*)

Sacu.   Cæsar, upon thy head
We citizens of Rome invoke the blessings   .

3*

Of all our Fathers' Gods.   We know that thou
Lovest the people, as thou lovest Rome.
    Cæs. Saculia, thanks!—and ye, kind friends and true.
Cæsar loves you ; and you, I know, love him.
And we love Rome—and strive to make her great,
And make her people prosper in their homes ;
So honest toil may meet its fair reward,
And honest parents happy children rear,
And not an honest man e'er beg in Rome.
    First Cit. That's the right kind of talk.   Hurra for
           Cæsar!
    Cits. Hurra for Cæsar!

        Enter ANTONY *with a king's crown.*

    Ant. Cæsar, thy legions love thee more than all
The rest of Rome can love thee; for they are
As thy own children.   On a hundred fields,
From Macedonia to farthest Gaul,
They've shared with thee the perils of stern war.
And thou hast ever cared for them, thy sons,
As if thou wert their father.   So they send
This golden crown, and pray that thou wouldst wear
It on thy sovereign brow until thou diest,
And be the mighty King of mighty Rome !

ANTONY *would put the crown on* CÆSAR's *head, but* CÆSAR
             will not suffer it.

    Sacu. Cæsar will wear no crown !   You see, my friends!
    Cits. Hurra for Cæsar !
    Cæs. (Rises.) Oh, Antony, how much thou wrongest
          Cæsar !
Go tell my legions I return their love
Even from this heart's core.   But tell my sons
That Cæsar says, Rome is no place for kings.
In this free Roman air kings cannot breathe !
Romans will never own a mortal king ;
They'll have no king but God !   Take thou this crown
Unto the Capitol, and place it there
Upon the mighty brows of Jupiter,
Great king of Gods and men !
    Ant. Cæsar, I will !   I stand rebuked before thee !
Thou art of the most ancient stock of Rome,
And worthy of thy fathers.   Citizens,

Let us record upon a plate of brass,
And place it here for after times to read,
That on this spot we offered mighty Cæsar
A kingly crown, and here his godlike words
Taught us our duty to himself and Rome.

Sacu. Mark Antony speaks well. Hurra for Antony!

Cits. Hurra for Antony!

Cæs. Let us proceed
To see the games. My Antony, thy arm.
Have that inscription placed without delay.

(*Exeunt* CÆSAR, ANTONY *and* CORNELIUS.)

Sacu. Come, friends, let's follow Cæsar to the games.
Hurra for Cæsar!

Cits. Hurra for Cæsar! (*Exeunt omnes.*)

END OF ACT IV.

ACT V.

THE DEATH OF CÆSAR.

SCENE I.—*Night. Room in the house of* CASSIUS.

Enter CASSIUS.

Cass. It is the hour, and yet not one has come.
Do their hearts fail them at the very last?

(*It thunders.*)

Perhaps the storm deters them. Men of straw
Alone would plead that bar. And yet such men
Make up the bulk o' the world; and we must work
With such material as the careless gods
Think well to furnish. Ah, here's one at last.

Enter DECIMUS.

Dec. Thy good health, Cassius. Where are all the rest?
It is a fearful night! Has no one come?

Cass. The storm no doubt detains them. Thou art here
Just on the hour, my Decimus.

Dec. Yes, trust me
For that. I'm an old soldier, Cassius.
When Cæsar set an hour, woe to the man,
However high his rank, who came too late.

Whate'er his faults, Cæsar's a general,
The pick of the whole world!
    Cass.   He's good enough.
But other men might be as good as he,
With equal chances.
    Dec.   Does our Brutus hold
Still to the bond? For we shall need him much;
The people have great faith in Marcus Brutus;
They think him honest above the common rule.
    Cass. The people are fools! They're taken with a show
A mere outside. Brutus puts on a face
Long as your arm—longer than Cato's even.
Talks loud of virtue, morals and all that.
Says he's a stoic—makes the people think
It is old Junius Brutus come again;
And after all—between us two, good Decimus—
He's but a solemn prig!
    Dec.   Do you think so?
    Cass. How did he make his fortune? I will tell you.
By lending money, at four per cent. a month,
To the Cilicians. Claudius was governor there—
Brutus had married Claudius's daughter—
His debtors could not pay. He marched an army,
And forced the money from them by the swords
Of Roman soldiers. Four per cent. a month!
There's usury for you! There's a stoic's morals!
    Dec. I had not heard of that. I was in Gaul.
    Cass. And just the other day, what does he do?
Tiring of Claudia, his wife—this stoic,
This proud despiser of all earthly joys,
Divorces her, and marries Portia,
His pretty cousin, stoic Cato's daughter!
There's morals for you! Get a name, my friend;
A good, strait, solemn mask; then you may punch
Old Bacchus in the ribs, and take your pleasure
Wherever you can find it.
    Dec.   Ah well, all men
Are pretty much alike. But, here is Brutus.

       Enter BRUTUS *and* CIMBER.

    Bru. A wild night this, brave Cassius.
    Cass.   All the better
To hide our meeting. Where's Trebonius?

Cim. Sickness detains him.   But he bade me say,
He will not fail you.   He is resolute
To overthrow the tyrant, or to die.

Bru. As we, the chiefs, must do the dangerous work,
Let's settle all our plans.   First, Cassius,
How many Senators are now enrolled
To aid us to the death?   Thou hast the list.

Cass. Full sixty Senators have set their names,
And pledged themselves to stand or fall together.

Bru. Has Cicero signed?

Cass.   I have not asked him, Brutus.
He is too old—too weak and wavering!
If tongues were swords, he'd be a mighty warrior.
But as it is, he's a mere piece of dough,
That'll stick to the winning side.

Bru. Now as to Antony and Lepidus.
Must they too die?

Cass.   I vote for Antony's death.
For Lepidus we needs must spare him, seeing
We cannot help it—being with his troops,
Outside the walls of the city.   Else I'd say,
Why, kill him too.

Bru.   Let us not rashly shed
A drop of needless blood.   They are but as
The vigorous arms of Cæsar.   When he dies,
The head drops off from all that mighty trunk.
The arms can then do nothing!

Cass.   No, not so.
Mark Antony's not Cæsar; but he is
A man of no slight mould.   Great Cæsar dwarfs him.
And there is also young Octavius.
He must not live.   I've weighed him well, my friends;
And mark my words, he'll prove a second Cæsar.

Dec. I do not go with you, good Cassius.
Mark Antony's not much.   I've fought with him,
And know the man.   And as for young Octavius,
I went with Cæsar and him, you know, to Spain—
All travelling together in one carriage.
He is not strong—a modest, kindly youth;
Not the least dangerous.

Bru.   Besides, you grant,
Wise Cassius, that we cannot easily reach
The man most to be dreaded, Lepidus; ·

Who has this moment under his command,
The only troops at Rome.   If we should kill
Mark Antony, he'll know he's only spared,
Because we could not strike him.   Thus we throw
Him and his soldiers 'gainst our noble cause
Just at the critical moment.   My advice
Is to spare Antony and Octavius too ;
And gain their aid by offers of promotion.
Get them to work on Lepidus, and thus
Prevent a struggle for supremacy,
Within the walls of Rome.   Cæsar once dead—
He's dead !   And vain, aspiring men like Antony
Will think far more of building up their fortunes,
Than of avenging that which cannot be
By mortal man undone.
   Dec.   Brutus is right.
My judgment goes with his.
   Cim.   And so does mine.
   Cass. So does not mine.   You will repeat, I fear,
Cæsar's own blunder.   For, had he not spared
Brutus and me, and fifty nobles more,
We should not now be plotting 'gainst his life.
   Bru. We owe to Cæsar gratitude, I grant.
And yet we owe a greater debt to Rome.
The smaller debt must yield before the greater.
Thus Junius Brutus—
   Cass. (*Aside.*)   Ye gods—he's started
On Junius Brutus !   When will he give o'er ?
   Bru. That great first Brutus, when he found his sons
Had joined with traitors to bring back false Tarquin,
And make him once more king ; he had them bound,
Brought to his judgment seat, and there, before
His own stern eyes, first scourged, then put to death !
'Twas like a Roman !   I would do the same.
Were Cæsar my own father, I would doom
Him to the death, Freedom to save and Rome !
   Cass. (*Aside.*) Yes, I believe he would.   He's as cold
                     blooded
As any fish !   I warrant that he knows
The half of Rome thiuk Cæsar *is* his father.
   Dec. Oh, gratitude claims nothing.   All the gifts
That Cæsar gives, belong to Rome, not him.
My mind is very easy on that score.

Cass. Of course I yield my judgment to you all.
I hope you'll not regret it.   Let that pass.
Now for the main plan.   Who will strike the blow—
The first, I mean?   We all will follow suit.
 Cim. I'm not much of a talker, so I'll do
My share in striking, if it please you all.
 Cass. Make up some story, Cimber.
 Cim.   Oh, that's easy.
I'll plead anew to gain my brother's pardon.   `
He will refuse me ; and be angry too,
Because I dare to press it.
 Cass.   Very good.
Then we will second you—and he will grow
Still angrier than before.   And then you'll strike.
 Dec. Who will take care of Antony?   He's a man
To give us trouble.
 Cass.   Ah, I've thought of that.
Trebonius must detain him at the door.
Offer to lend him money—that will keep him.
For Antony is always wanting money ;
Always would want it, were he governor
Of half the provinces.
 Bru.   What more's to plan ?
 Cass. I think of nothing.
 Dec.   Nor I. (*Goes to window.*)   See,
                              morning breaks !
 Bru. We'd better part at once.   The storm is fled.
 Cass. That storm's blown by ; a greater lies ahead !
                    (*Exeunt* BRUTUS, DECIMUS *and* CIMBER.)
 Cass. What fools men are ; how they delude themselves !
Now I know what I do, and what I mean.
Cæsar has injured me.   He seized the lions
I'd purchased for my games, and left at Megara.
That's one offence.   Then when I made petition
For the first Prætorship, he owned that I
Deserved it most, having done Rome most service ;
But gave it all the same to Marcus Brutus,
Who had done naught, because forsooth he loved him !
He may love Brutus, but I'll prove this day,
By Brutus' sword, what Brutus' love is worth.
Brutus ! he is my tool !—this wondrous Brutus
Of whom Rome thinks so highly !   He might be,
Next to great Cæsar, the first man in Rome.

And, after Cæsar's death, the very first;
For Cæsar loves him as he might his son.
Were Cassius Brutus, I would sooner die
Than wound the man who loved me in that sort.
But then I'm no philosopher; my eyes
Are fixed on earth, not wandering in the skies.

(Exit CASSIUS.)

SCENE II.—*Room in* CÆSAR'S *house.*

Enter CÆSAR *and* CORNELIUS.

Cor. I also counsel, Cæsar, 'gainst thy going.
Nothing is lost by staying, nothing risked.
In such a case, why not remain at home?
Cæs. Only because I will not live in fear.
Cæsar would rather die this very day
Than live in constant dread of any foe.
I should have died a hundred deaths ere this,
In my campaigns in Gaul, in Greece, in Spain,
If I had given myself the least concern
About my safety.   Why am I here now?
Because the great gods ordered I should live,
To do their work in Rome.   When that is done,
And it is best for Rome that I should die,
Then all the swords of all my friends would fail
To save me from my foes.   Cornelius,
I have no dread of death.   The doom the gods
Have made the fate of all, or soon or late,
Cannot be bad for man.   What's natural,
Cannot be evil.   As for me, I feel
Like one whose work is done; and to whom rest,
In this world or the shades, were now the great,
Yes, the supremest blessing!

Enter ANTONY.

Ant. Stir not from home this morning, mighty Cæsar!
There is a plot on foot.   I'm sure of it.
I hear the whispers of conspiracy
On every side.   Treason is in the air.
Men shake their heads and mutter as I pass.
Stir not a step from home without a guard
Of thy old soldiers.   They can not be bought.

Cæs. I'm sick of all this talk of plots and treason.
See, here's a letter has been sent to me,
Or, rather, to Cornelius.   (*Takes out letter.*)
               Here's a list
Of sixty of the noblest names in Rome.
Among them Brutus; yes, the man I love
Above all other men—because, because
His mother was my friend, my dearest friend
Of all the women in Rome. And Decimus,
Who fought with me in Gaul—the officer
I trusted next to thee, my Antony.
And Cassius, who, although he loves me not,
Accepted life and honors from my hand.
Why, even thou, my Antony, art accused;
And Lepidus. And why not also you,
If all the rest are faithless? By the gods,
If all the world be made up thus of knaves,
If there be none Cæsar can longer trust,
Why then his time has surely come to die;
Yes, and far happier then to die than live!
    Ant. Well, take thy guards! That I am true, I prove
By giving thee such counsel.
    Cæs.   Antony!
When I believe that thou, my friend, art false,
Death will be more than welcome.
               Enter SOOTHSAYER.
    Sooth. Great Cæsar, go not forth from home to-day.
In offering up the morning's sacrifice,
I've found a yearling calf that has no heart.
It is most inauspicious, dire and dreadful!
The gods say to thee, Cæsar, go not forth!
    Cæs. It is not wondrous calves should have no hearts,
If all the noblest men in Rome have none.
But I should think that if the gracious gods
Had any word for Cæsar, they would send it
Direct to him in visions or in dreams.
For me, I never felt more calm a mind
Than I do now, when I have schooled my soul
To meet what fate the mighty gods ordain.
    Sooth. The night was terrible. The lightning smote
The turrets of thy house. Roarings were heard,
As if of lions, in the empty streets.
Men fought in the skies. Earth shook. Red meteors

Crashed down within the Forum, smiting there
Thy statue to the pavement.
    Cæs.   And all this
Portends great harm to me?
    Sooth.   Most surely, Cæsar.
    Cæs. And if I stay at home, I shall escape?
    Sooth. Of course. How else?
    Cæs.   Why then it seems to me
The mighty gods have ta'en great trouble for naught.
All this mad strain of the wild elements
To keep one man at home! Why a mere rind
Of melon placed beneath my hasty foot,
Had better done the work at trifling cost.
    Sooth. Cæsar, respect the gods—the ordaining gods!
    Cæs. I do respect them more than thou canst know—
When they decree that Cæsar's time has come
To leave this world, then naught that he can do,
Or going or staying, will that doom avert.
A Persian monarch once, in grievous fear,
Went to a wise Magician. "Shield me now
From harm this day; it is my day of doom.
Send me by thy great power to the world's end;
And name thy own reward." The Magian did.
That afternoon the dreadful angel Death,
Came also to the Magian. "Where goest thou?"
Said the Magician. "I am bound straightway,"
Replied stern Death, "unto the end o' the world;
Where it was doomed one thousand years ago,
Thy monarch should await me." Such is Fate!
No art can baffle, and no sacrifice
Change the resolve of the eternal gods.
All man can do, is calmly to submit.
    Sooth. Well, I have done my duty by thee, Cæsar.
                         (*Exit* SOOTHSAYER.)

Enter CALPURNIA.

    Cal. Oh, Cæsar, thou must not go forth to-day!
I pray thee, go not! I, Calpurnia,
Thy wedded wife, beg this one favor of thee.
I could not sleep last night—the door flew open,
Without a cause. There was no one without.
Then, near the morn, at last I fell asleep.
And then I dreamed—(*Clasps her hands.*)

Cæs.   What didst thou dream, Calpurnia?
Cal. I cannot tell thee, Cæsar!
Cæs.   Fear thou not
It will alarm me. I can show perhaps,
It has but little meaning.
     Cal. I heard the fierce, vindictive tread of foes
Approaching through the empty corridor.
It echoed through my dream. The door flew wide.
There was a gleam of swords. And then I held
A murdered body close within my arms.
The blood was streaming from a hundred wounds.
I could not see the face, although I strove
With all my might, as we oft do in dreams.
Then like a flash, my eyelids sprang apart,
And I beheld thy face!   (*She seems about to faint.*)
     Cæs. (*Catches her in his arms.*) My sweet Calpurnia!
     Cal. Thou wilt not go to-day? Grant me but this!
'Tis the first favour I e'er asked of thee.
And, if thou goest, the last! Thou wilt not go?
     Cæs. I will not. Friends, I shall remain at home.
Not that I fear, but that Calpurnia fears.
     Cal. Thanks, Cæsar, thanks! A weight is off my heart!
I will not trouble further. Worthy friends,
Good-day!
     Cæs.   One kiss, my love! When Cæsar dies,
His chiefest grief will be to part from thee!
                (*Kisses her. Exit* CALPURNIA.)
     Ant. I also will go now, since thou art safe.
                    (*Exit* ANTONY.)
     Cor. 'Twould be a good occasion to review
Those letters I have written.
     Cæs.   No, not to-day,
My dear old friend. I'm ill at heart to-day.

            Enter DECIMUS.

     Dec. Cæsar, the Senate waits thee.
     Cæs.   Decimus,
I have resolved to bide at home to-day.
     Dec. Why, how is this? Thou saidst thou would be
         there;
And Cæsar's word was never like a vane
Which veers from North to South ev'n while we gaze.
     Cæs. The omens are unfavourable.

Dec. (Laughs.)   The omens!
What! Cæsar, too, is growing superstitious!
I well remember when thou wast in Gaul,
Fighting the Celts, those children of the night,
The Augurs said the entrails of a sheep
Forbade the battle.   And that Cæsar said,
" 'Twas not to be supposed a silly sheep
Could know the hour that it was best to fight
So well as an old soldier."   Then all laughed.
Cæs. (Laughs.) Yes, I remember that.   And Decimus
What's more, we won the battle!   Dost thou know,
Of all my deeds, I pride me most on Gaul?
As Cicero told the Senate, 'twas not merely
Another Province gained; but that a cloud
Was now dispersed, which had o'erhung the State
Since the sad days when Brennus and his Gauls
Stormed madly into Rome.   But it required
Hard fighting—did it not, my Decimus?
Dec. Ah, those were glorious days!
Cæs.   ⋆   Indeed they were.
And dost remember, my brave Decimus,
How, at that very battle, thou and I
Rallied the Tenth, my favorite legionaries;
Seizing their standard, telling them the foe
Lay just the other way—until for shame
They ceased their flight, and turned defeat to glory?
Dec. Yes, I remember well.   But 'twas thy work!
I saw thee—dressed in scarlet, with bared head—
Flashing like Mars before the runaways,
Filling their hearts anew with life and hope,
And making them invincible!   Yes, in truth,
It was thy victory, Cæsar.   All I did
Was naught compared with thee.
Cæs.   And then again,
When we two fought in Spain.   That *was* a fight,
That last at Munda.   Arméd hand to hand,
And foot to foot.   'Twas Roman then to Roman!
Ah, we have seen great deeds, we two, together.
Strange how my mind doth wander off of late,
' To the old days—our victories, and reverses.
For Fortune wills, my friend, like a coy maid,
To hide herself at times from ev'n her lovers;
To be won back by importunities,

And make her doubly sweet.
        But thou cam'st, Decimus,
To take me to the Senate. I would go,
Only I promised my Calpurnia
To bide at home to-day. She had a dream
That moved her much last night.
  Dec.   That is a pity!
For 'tis arranged to take a final vote
On thy new laws to-day ;—the laws to drain
The Pontine Marshes, and improve the Tiber.
If thou'rt not there, I fear the laws may fail.
But 'tis the way o' the world. A woman's dream
Often has swayed far greater plans than these.
What must be must. And yet one little hour
Would serve to work no common good to Rome.
  Cæs. When I decided, I knew not my laws
Were now before the Senate. Else I had
Come to a different judgment. When Duty calls,
'Tis Cæsar's part to go ; nor ask what dreams,
Dangers, or omens seek to bar the way.
  Cor. I thought it settled that thou wouldst not go.
Calpurnia thought so. Were it not then well
To beg the Senate to postpone their vote
Until to-morrow?
  Dec.   'Twere an unwise move.
'Twould cause dissatisfaction ; no good reason
For Cæsar's absence given.
  Cæs.   Peace, good friends!
When I resolved to stay, I did not know
There were such weighty reasons for my going.
If dangerous to-day, why not to-morrow?
Cornelius, tell my wife Calpurnia—
Nay! it is best that thou shouldst hold thy peace,
And tell her nothing. It will save her pain.
In a few hours I shall again return,
If 't please the gracious gods, before she knows
I have been absent. Come, good Decimus!
Cornelius, a few words with thee, my friend.
       (*Exeunt* CÆSAR *and* CORNELIUS.)
  Dec. So goes the lion where the hunters lie!
Cæsar, the hour has come that thou must die!
I am a villain, and I know it well ;
But I'll be first in Rome, if lowest in hell! (*Exit* DECIMUS.)

SCENE III.—*Pompey's Portico, with Statue of Pompey.*

CICERO *and* SENATORS *at back of stage, seated.* BRUTUS,
      CASSIUS, CASCA *and* CIMBER *in front.*

Bru. (*To Cass.*) Perhaps he will not come. Where's
                  Decimus ?

Cass. He's gone to bring him.

Bru.   Not an easy task,
If Cæsar wills to stay. And yet though rude
At times to some, he's always kind to him—
His old companion in so many wars.

Cass. Oh, Cæsar has his little weaknesses,
Like other men. I knew a cunning lure
Would bring him here to-day. There are few locks
That some key will not open.

Bru.   What lure was that ?

Cass. The story that the Senate's now to vote
On his new laws.

Bru.   But, as it is not so,
He'll find he's been deceived—and know at once
Some mischief is intended.

Cass.   We must strike
Therefore at once. Cimber, thou know'st thy part ?

Cim. I'll anger him, and then will pull his gown
From off his shoulder. Casca then will strike.

Cass. Thou wilt not fear him, Casca ?

Casca.   No, not I !
I killed a lion once with one sharp thrust.

Cass. Well, think he is a lion, and strike home.
Avoid his eyes, though.

Casca.   Oh, I'll strike him quick,
And from behind. He'll turn, you know, on Cimber,
And then I'll strike him.

Cass.   And then all must strike.
Thou wilt not fail us, Brutus ? Every steel
Must redden with his blood, to show that all
Have taken part in this.

Bru.   I will not fail.
Brutus shall do his part in freeing Rome,
Whate'er the end may be.

Cass.   Hush ! here he comes !

Enter CÆSAR *and* DECIMUS. SENATORS *rise from their*

Cæs. Be seated, Senators! (*Comes forward.*)
Good morning, friends!
Brutus, thou'rt well? Ah, noble Cassius!
And Casca—and thou, Cimber. Hail to all!
(*He takes his seat.*)

Cim. Hail, mighty Cæsar! I would ask a favor.

Cæs. Cimber, proceed! If 'tis in Cæsar's power,
It shall be done. Does it concern Bithynia,
Thy province?

Cim. I would once again implore,
Oh, mighty Cæsar, pardon for my brother!

Cæs. Cimber, thou vexest me!—to ask for that
Which is not mine to give. Thy brother's deeds
Were fitly punished with the avenging sword.
Yet he is simply banished. Say no more.
I will not hear thee. Hast thou not a province?
Surely, I have been generous to thee.

Casca. I second noble Cimber, mighty Cæsar!
Grant him his wish. I pray thee on my knees!
(*He kneels.*)

Cæs. Rise, Casca—you offend me! Romans should
Kneel only to the gods!

Cass. (*Sneeringly.*) Thou mak'st thyself
Great as a god. Therefore men kneel to thee.

Cæs. (*Indignant.*) Cassius! What meanest thou? Such
shameless words
Are not to be o'erlooked. (*Cæsar rises.*)

Cim. Keep thou thy seat,
Thou cruel tyrant!

(CIMBER *pulls back* CÆSAR'S *robe off his shoulder.*)

Cæs. What! How dar'st thou, Cimber?

Casca. Down with the tyrant! (*Stabs Cæsar from behind.*)

Cæs. (*Seizes Casca's arm.*) Villain! Thou shalt die!

Casca. (*Frightened.*) Help, brothers—help!

Cim. I'll die then too! (*He stabs.*)

Cæs. Oh, thou ungrateful wretch!

(*Turns upon* CIMBER, *who struggles with him.*)

Cass. I'll make another, Cæsar! (*Cass. stabs him.*)

Cæs. Cassius—and thou!
This is thy thanks—because I spared thy life;

And made thee Prætor ; and then gave to thee
A noble province !
     (CÆSAR *stands as if faint from his wounds.*)
  Cass. (*To Bru.*) Why stand'st thou aloof?
Dost thou forget thy promise?
  Bru.   Die, tyrant ! Die!
                     (*He stabs Cæsar.*)
  Cæs. (*Starts—and looks at Brutus.*) And thou too,
      Brutus !

   (CÆSAR *reels, and falls at base of Pompey's statue.*)

  Cass. He's dead ! Yes, dead at murdered Pompey's feet.
Great Pompey is avenged !
  Bru.   Now let us haste
To take possession of the Capitol.
  Cass. And as we go, we'll cry, The Tyrant's dead !
And Rome is free ! Come, brave Conspirators !

Exeunt CONSPIRATORS, *flourishing their weapons, and crying
   out "The Tyrant's dead!" " Rome is Free!"*

SENATORS *run out alarmed before them, except* CICERO, *who
  hides behind a column—and then comes forward to body of*
  CÆSAR.

  Cic. Oh, mighty Julius ! liest thou here so still !
One hour ago thy forehead awed the world.
The wide earth rocked beneath thee like a boat,
When thou didst step from one side to the other.
And now thou'rt gone ! Where has thy spirit gone?
  Sacu. (*Outside.*) Vengeance upon the murderers ! Let
                us storm
The Capitol ! Send word to Lepidus
To bring the troops. Kill all !
  Cit. (*Outside.*) Kill ! kill the murderers !
  Cic. (*Listening.*)   The mob is up !
They howl like wolves upon a bloody track !
Thy spirit, mighty Cæsar, rules us still !

           END OF ACT V.

www.ingramcontent.com/pod-product-compliance
Lightning Source LLC
Chambersburg PA
CBHW030015030726
47499CB00008B/3009